Footsteps. Furtive footsteps . . .

To Bethany's horror, the footsteps were pounding toward her. The man lunged, his hands outstretched, fingers spread wide apart.

She screamed, clutching at the edge of the wall. A rough hand clamped about her arm; another grabbed her coat, jerking her so hard that her teeth closed with a loud snap. Kicking out wildly, she felt her foot catch him in the shin. When he stumbled, she slammed her fist into his face.

"Stop it!" he exploded, pushing her down against the cold cement.

She flung her body back and forth, flailing frantically in an effort to break free. The man fell heavily across her knees and leaned forward to press one hand tightly over her mouth, cutting off her screams.

"Listen, I don't know what your problem is," he said flatly, "but suicide isn't the answer."

CALL OF THE DOVE

Madge Harrah

Serenade/Serenata BOOKS
of the Zondervan Publishing House
Grand Rapids, Michigan

CALL OF THE DOVE
Copyright © 1985 by Madge Harrah

Serenade/Serenata is an imprint of
The Zondervan Publishing House
1415 Lake Drive, S.E.
Grand Rapids, MI 49506

ISBN 0-310-46852-3

Edited by Anne Severance
Designed by Kim Koning

Printed in the United States of America

85 86 87 88 89 90 / 10 9 8 7 6 5 4 3 2 1

To Larry
Then, now, and always

CHAPTER 1

FOOTSTEPS. FURTIVE FOOTSTEPS. Leather shuffling stealthily against concrete.

The sound coursed through Bethany like an electric shock. She lifted her head to peer sideways through her long thick lashes. Her breath caught in her throat when she spied a tall, dark-haired man in a blue windbreaker and jeans lurking near the southeast corner of the parapet. Although he quickly turned his head away, she got the distinct feeling he'd been watching her.

How long had she leaned there against the four-foot wall surrounding the observation platform with her face buried in her arms? A couple minutes, at least.

She straightened, lifting one hand to brush tangled strands of long blond hair back from her amber flecked green eyes. Her tan raincoat fluttered about her slender body like a wind-whipped flag. She continued to watch the man from the corner of her eye. He stood motionless, a dark silhouette against the gray clouds.

Idiot—you should never have come up here alone! Bethany scolded herself.

She'd assumed the walkway would be crowded with other sightseers who would have traveled to the top of the thirty-story-high City Hall, even as she had that Saturday afternoon in April, to take in the view. It was a grand sight from that vantage point, with office buildings, flower-filled parks, boulevards, freeways and railroad yards sprawling in all directions toward the horizon where church spires and radio towers pinned earth to sky. The Missouri River, a snake with wind-silvered scales, slithered out of the plains to loop itself about the town.

Contrary to Bethany's expectations, however, she'd found the walkway deserted. Isolated so high above the city, she'd been overwhelmed by a sudden yearning for someone with whom to share the view, a man—a special man—handsome and strong, to savor with her the scented spring air, the delicate fragrance of redbud and daffodil.

Spring, the season for lovers. In the "City of Romance." That's what she'd heard Kansas City was called, with more fountains than any other city in the world except Rome, more boulevards than any other city except Paris. But where was her "special someone," a man who would see her as a person, a companion to be cherished, not as a casual conquest or a modern day "score?" Terrible word, *score,* as though love were a game, not a God-given treasure.

Earlier, wandering alone down the flower-fringed boulevards, she'd decided, on impulse, to try the view from the top of City Hall, hoping it would cheer her up. It hadn't. With her head buried in her arms on the parapet wall, she'd sent a prayer winging toward the clouds above: *Dear Lord, please help. I'm so lonely! Surely there's someone in this town for me, someone I can love. When I see him, could You give me some kind of sign . . . ?*

But was God listening? Bethany wasn't sure, not anymore. Her faith, once strong, had lately teetered on a precipice of doubt, a cliff as sheer as the drop from this high building—

That's when she heard the soft footsteps and glanced up to see the tall dark man watching her with that intense look. Scenes from several television shows flipped through her mind—a girl beaten by a stranger in an alley, a woman pushed from a cliff during a struggle with an attacker—

She edged away while trying to estimate how far it might be around the walkway to the door on the other side. This top floor, designed strictly for storage, had been indented to leave space for the encircling concrete platform. Windowless, with thick gray walls, it provided a barrier through which cries for help would not penetrate to the floors below.

Reaching the corner, Bethany glanced back to see if the man were still in the same place. With raw fear burning her throat, she saw that he was moving toward her and that he was staring at her again. For one split second she looked directly into his black eyes, deep-set beneath thick, dark brows. A mistake, she told herself angrily. She should never have allowed herself to make eye contact with him. Now he would think she was inviting his approach. She hurried around the corner, hoping that someone else might be there, after all. Instead, the walkway stretched before her, bleak and empty, like the battlement of a deserted castle. As she stumbled along, she wondered how many people might have jumped or been pushed from this spot in the past. The building fell away below the parapet in a streamlined shaft, with only two narrow ledges to stop a plummeting body. Her artist's eye painted the picture for her in lurid detail—she saw herself hurtling through the air, heard the thud when she hit the marble steps in front of the building, saw her body lying crumpled near the famous City Hall fountains where copper-green horses and dolphins sprayed water from open mouths into foaming concrete channels.

She stopped for a moment, listening intently. Maybe the man had left. Maybe the threat of rain had proved too much for him and he'd gone back downstairs. . . . Suddenly she was struck by another thought: What if he had run around the other way? What if he were waiting to grab her beyond the next corner?

She looked frantically back and forth, trying to decide which direction to take. At the same time, a voice within told her to stop acting so foolish. The man was probably harmless, a tourist enjoying the view. She was letting her imagination get the best of her.

When the man did not appear, Bethany decided he had indeed left the platform. She moved back to the parapet and took a sketch pad and pencil from her tan canvas tote bag. Opening to a clean page, she began slashing across it with swift strokes, trying to capture the energy of the scene before her: buildings angling up from the streets below, sharply defined in the downtown area, but dissolving into a hazy vagueness where the soft gray clouds unfurled a veil of rain.

Not bad, she decided, holding the sketch at arms' length. Maybe she could work it up in some way as a Christmas card—change the rain to snow, put decorations on the buildings, lights in the windows, Santa's sleigh appearing out of the clouds. Would her supervisor at the King Card Company go for it? she wondered. Might be worth a try. Surely he wouldn't limit her to designing sympathy cards forever. Birthday cards—now *that's* what she'd really like to do.

She put the pad down on top of the wall and dug in her tote bag for a sharper pencil. A sudden gust of wind ruffled the pages of the pad, skidding it around and pushing it off the wall into space. Instinctively, forgetting the danger, Bethany lunged forward to grab for the pad. But in vain.

To her horror, she heard heavy footsteps pounding toward her.

She whipped her head around in time to see the nightmare become reality—the man was already upon her, his hands outstretched, fingers spread. Bethany screamed, clutching at the edge of the wall. A rough hand clamped around her arm, another grabbed her coat, jerking her so hard that her teeth closed with a loud snap. She tried to twist from the man's grasp, but he held on tight. Kicking out wildly, she felt her foot catch him in the shin. When he stumbled, she slammed her fist into his face.

"Stop it!" he exploded, pushing her down on her back against the cold cement.

She flung her body back and forth, flailing frantically in an effort to break free. The man fell heavily across her knees and leaned forward to press one

11

hand tight over her mouth, cutting off her screams. "Listen, I don't know what your problem is," he said flatly, "but suicide isn't the answer, believe me."

She stopped struggling and lay still, staring up at him in shocked disbelief. He continued to hold her tightly while riveting her with an earnest look.

"Life can be hard, but that pavement down there is even harder. It's a messy way to go," he continued.

When she still didn't move, he slowly took his hand from her mouth and rolled off her knees, but he kept a grip on her arm. She could see, now, that his eyes were blue. They had looked black because they'd been shadowed by his thick black brows. His face was lean with a strong jaw. Several curly black locks of hair had fallen down over his forehead in the struggle. He reached to brush them back, leaving them in tangled disarray.

"You thought I was going to jump!" Bethany said in amazement. Even though he had now released his hold, she felt he would pounce if she made one false move. Slowly she pushed herself up on her elbows. "Thanks for trying to save my life, but you've made a mistake—"

He shook his head, interrupting her. "You're too young and pretty to say a thing like that."

She realized with dismay that he still misunderstood her.

"No, I wasn't going to jump," she argued—too loudly. Even to her own ears, her protest sounded false. She tried again. "You see, I thought . . ." She choked on a brief laugh. *And that*, she told herself angrily, *sounded hysterical*. Taking a deep breath, she forced herself to speak in a normal voice. "I thought you were going to *push* me."

She felt a surge of dismay at how crazy those words might seem to him.

"What I mean to say is—what I mean . . . ," she stammered, shaking her head in frustration. "You must think I'm really stupid—maybe even irrational."

He continued to study her face. She could see he didn't trust her. "I'm used to it," he said dryly.

"Used to stupidity?"

"To irrational statements." He did not smile. His eyes were windows, a clear bright blue, gleaming with light.

Uncomfortable under that blue scrutiny, Bethany gathered the contents that had spilled from her bag and then climbed awkwardly to her feet. She straightened her coat, wincing at the pain that suddenly shot through her right shoulder. Frowning, she kneaded her upper arm.

The man had risen, too, and now stood before her, a good six inches taller than her 5'7". He looked lithe but strong, as though he might be a soccer player, or maybe a runner. Glancing down, she saw that he did have on jogging shoes.

"You're rubbing your arm—are you hurt?" he asked.

Looking back at his face, she realized with relief that some of the intensity had left his eyes. Although he did appear to be truly concerned, he no longer fixed her with that unnerving gaze.

"I think I've pulled a muscle." She lifted her other arm to rub the back of her head. She laughed once, a short laugh, as she felt the knot there that was already the size of a small plum. "And a bump on the head. How's your leg?"

Demonstrating a total lack of self-consciousness, he peeled up the left leg of his jeans, exposing his shin. Bethany saw a red mark where she'd kicked him. The spot would undoubtedly soon turn into an ugly bruise. He stood up, shrugging ruefully. "One wound for two."

"No, we're even," she told him, "because you're also going to have a black eye."

He tentatively touched the swelling on his left cheek. Suddenly he grinned. The change in his expression gave him the countenance of a mischievous boy. "We had a dandy fight going there for a while."

Welcoming the lighter mood, Bethany tried again to explain. "Look . . . what happened was I dropped my sketch pad and tried to catch it. I wasn't going to jump."

"Occupational response on my part," he said, shaking his head as though reproving himself. "I'm sorry for tackling you like that. Maybe I need a vacation."

"What is it you do, Mr.—?" She let the last word trail away while she waited for him to supply a name.

"Rosselli. Dr. Shaun Rosselli. I work at Henderson Hospital."

The children's mental health clinic. . . . That explained everything, Bethany thought, remembering how she'd been leaning against the parapet with her head in her arms when he'd first seen her. She must indeed have looked dangerously depressed. No wonder he'd drawn the wrong conclusion.

"I owe you an apology, too," she said. "I'd decided you were a—a . . . " She paused, unable to say the word.

"A threat to the virtue of women?" he finished wryly. Lifting both hands, he tried once more, without success, to straighten his hair. All he did was make things worse. "Maybe I'll shave it all off. What do you think—would I look less frightening if I were bald?"

He fixed her again with those intense blue eyes, pulling his black brows together in a quizzical frown. She sketched him in her mind, leaving off the hair. With that strong, tight-jawed face and those blue, searchlight eyes, he turned out to be disturbingly handsome, even without hair.

"You'd look just fine," she announced, "and not at all frightening."

He exhaled as though relieved and gave her a big grin. "Whew, that's good! Most of the men in my family lose their hair by the age of forty. I have ten years to go." Stepping to the parapet, he glanced down the wall. "With this wind, your sketchbook may be halfway to St. Louis by now. Still, it's worth a look. Let's go down and see what we can find."

He reached to take her arm. But she sensed something a little patronizing, something clinical, in his attitude, which made her step away.

"You're still not sure about me, are you?" she asked flatly.

Sobering, he gave her a straight look. "Analyzing people is my business and it isn't hard to see there's something bothering you. Do me a favor, will you, and come downstairs with me, so I won't have to worry about you?"

She gazed into those amazing blue eyes in that craggy face and felt a quickening of her pulse. He had the rough-hewn strength of a pioneer, of a man who could fell a forest or track a bear. At the same time there was a gentleness about him, a contrast that intrigued her. She wondered, for one brief moment, what it might be like to kiss him, to have those arms that had held her in a bruising grip such a short time before entwine about her in a tender embrace. But such speculation was foolish. He'd soon say goodbye and that would be the end of it.

She tore her gaze away, listening to the return of the wind as it swooped around the corner, like a child playing Hide and Seek, now trying to reach home base. It whirled past, and Bethany imagined she could hear it calling, "Allee, allee, in free!"

She envied the wind, for she was not free and hadn't been for a long time. How had he been able to see into her mind, to pick up on the hurt that she tried so diligently to hide from those around her? It was only one small haunted corner where childhood memories, impossible to suppress, sometimes emerged from the shadows. A man that perceptive was something she'd often dreamed about. Now, however, she felt uneasy beneath his penetrating gaze. She forced a smile to her face, to cover whatever flicker of expression might reveal that he'd struck closer to the mark than was comfortable.

"Thanks for being concerned, but I'm fine," she said brightly, hoping she sounded convincing.

He tilted his head and grinned at her with one eyebrow cocked.

"Well, the least I can do after knocking you down is offer you a cup of coffee. How about it?"

"You don't have to do th—"

"I'd like to," he interrupted. "Or would you prefer an ice cream cone? I happen to be hooked on butter pecan ice cream. Fattening, of course, but I don't think you have to worry about that; your figure looks perfect to me. Speaking strictly as a doctor, of course."

He gave her a mock lecherous leer, which might have come straight out of an oldtime melodrama. She had to laugh; she couldn't help it.

"That's better," he said, nodding with approval. "So what will it be, coffee or ice cream?"

"Coffee, very hot and very black."

"You got it."

They descended in the elevator to the lobby and walked together past the statue of George Washington and through the revolving doors out onto the steps. The sun broke through the scudding clouds to throw shafts of golden light over the rearing horses and dolphins in the fountains below.

"Where are you parked?" the man asked.

"I didn't drive. I took the bus today."

"Good. That simplifies things," he replied. "My car is in that lot across the street—"

"Wait a minute," Bethany broke in. "I thought we were just going to get a cup of coffee around here somewhere. I really don't know you . . ."

He nodded. "You're wise to be careful. Here . . . my I.D."

He pulled a battered wallet from his pocket and opened it to show his driver's license. As Bethany peered through the plastic envelope holding the card, he intoned, "Shaun Churchill Rosselli, six-foot-two, black hair, blue eyes, one hundred eighty pounds."

"Shaun *Churchill* Rosselli?" she asked, grinning at the incongruity of his names.

"Sure," he answered matter-of-factly. "Shaun is in

honor of my Irish mother; Churchill, for her English grandfather; and Rosselli for my Italian father. Just call me Shaun.''

Now Bethany laughed out loud. ''Irish, English and Italian—that's some combination. And it still doesn't prove I'd be safe with you.''

He grimaced, clutching at his head. ''It's the hair! I know it's the hair! If I were bald, you'd trust me!''

He turned to another leaf in the plastic folder. ''Here, this ought to do it. My membership card in the American Psychological Association.''

Just as she'd suspected—a man who could look deeply into the feelings of others. She wasn't sure she wanted to be around someone who might keep analyzing everything she said or did. On the other hand, she felt strangely warmed by his lack of conceit, his open laughing face.

Making her decision, she said, ''All right. Where shall we go?''

''Chandler Court. You know—that sidewalk café in Country Club Plaza? The coffee there is excellent.''

Bethany's pulse quickened. The Country Club Plaza, with its quaint shops, splashing fountains, tiled grottos and imported statues, was one of her favorite places in the entire city.

''So what do I call you?'' he asked.

''My name's Bethany Clark, but I'll answer to Beth. Or Bet. Or B.C.''

''B.C.? And you thought Churchill was strange?'' he remarked with a teasing grin. ''I like the name Bethany—it has a nice ring to it. Come on, Bethany, let's find your sketch book.''

They proceeded down the steps to the sidewalk below. The water splashing in the fountains sounded like a woodland rill. They moved between the spilling channels to the end of the walk and then made their way back over the grass to the west side of the building.

"It's hopeless!" Bethany exclaimed when she looked about at the wind-blown trash caught in the shrubbery.

"Could be, but we'll never know what we'll find until we try," Shaun replied cheerfully. He began poking at various pieces of paper. Suddenly he bent and plucked a torn sheet that dangled like a flower from a thorny limb. "Hey, is this yours?"

She joined him and saw that he held a portion of a pencil sketch she'd made the night before. The sketch pictured a freckle-faced boy with a cocker spaniel.

"Yes, I was working on a birthday card idea . . . " She saw the questioning look on his face and explained, "I'm an artist with the King Card Company."

"You're very good," he commented thoughtfully. "That child's face—it reminds me of a boy I'm working with at the clinic."

He lifted his eyes, blazing at her with a look of such brilliance that she had a giddy feeling, as though she were plunging forward into a pool of light.

"You may be the person I've been searching for!" he announced.

"Wh—what do you mean?" she stammered. She took a deep breath, trying to slow her pounding pulse.

He continued to hold her with that astonishing blue gaze. "I'll tell you over coffee. Until then—you'll just have to wonder."

He took her arm in his and her heart thudded at his touch. As she hurried along, trying to match his long-legged stride, she peered up at his craggy jaw, his wind-tangled hair, and remembered the prayer she had whispered just before he had appeared—a prayer that God would send her someone to love. Could this man be the answer to that plea? Her blood sang in her veins, sparkling like an effervescent spring of fresh water touched by sunlight. For this moment, at least, the haunting voices from her childhood kept their silence.

CHAPTER 2

DURING THE DRIVE TO THE PLAZA, Bethany continued to watch Shaun from the corner of her eye. His hands on the steering wheel looked sensitive, yet the bruises on her arms attested to the strength in his fingers. He radiated male power, a kind of energy, that made her breath catch in her throat. What did he sense? What did those blue eyes see?

Bethany found herself pulling her left hand and wrist up inside the sleeve of her coat to hide the almost invisible scars that laced the flesh like a pale spiderweb.

He parked in the Plaza Central lot. They then left the car and walked around the corner to Nichols Road where they passed the alcove holding the Pool of Four Fauns. There, on the white marble bench against the west wall, sat a boy and girl gazing into each other's eyes as if transfixed. Shaun's fingers tightened around Bethany's arm. She risked a quick glance toward his face and found him smiling down at her with an expression that seemed to hold a challenge. She could tell that he'd noticed the lovers, too.

Warmth rose from her neck toward her cheeks and she glanced away to hide the blush, forcing herself to focus on the red, yellow and blue tile mosaic that zigzagged up the walls of the Plaza Medical Building across the street. Atop the building perched a tall cupola with Moorish arches and a red-tiled roof while beyond loomed the Giralda Tower, another Moorish fantasy crowned with statues.

"There's something magical about this place," she commented. "It's like a picture from a fairy tale—all these lacy balconies, the fountains, the hidden gardens. J. C. Nichols must have spent a fortune on it."

"He was an amazing man, all right," Shaun agreed. Bethany sensed that he understood her recent confusion and was trying to put her at ease. Speaking in a casual tone, he went on: "He imported the fountains and statues from Europe to make the Plaza as beautiful as possible when he built it back in the Twenties. He was truly a man of vision. Did you know this was the first shopping center in America?"

He continued to talk about the Plaza until they reached Chandler Court. Bethany had been afraid they might get caught in a rain shower, but the sun, which had been teasing the last of the clouds, now broke through in full force, flinging brilliant sparkles over the streams of water that spilled from the Fountain of Pan. Shaun held the wrought-iron gate for Bethany to pass through into the courtyard, then followed her, indicating a table near the fountains.

Now that the sun was out and the wind had died down a bit, Bethany decided to remove her raincoat. Shaun stepped forward at once to help her. As he draped her coat over a chair, Bethany was glad that she had worn a soft blue wool skirt and matching cashmere sweater instead of the usual jeans and pullover. When Shaun removed his own jacket and sat down in a chair opposite her, Bethany started with surprise at the sight of a silver cross suspended from a chain about his neck.

Shaun glanced down at the cross, following her gaze, then up again. "Is something wrong?"

"No, I—I just didn't expect to find a psychologist wearing *that*. I guess I thought you were all . . . "

"Atheists?" he finished for her.

"I guess so."

He laughed. "I don't know why we get such a bad press."

"But I knew a psychology major back in college who said religion was a crutch—"

"It can be," he interrupted in a matter-of-fact voice, "if that's what you make it. Or it can be a great help."

She looked at him uncertainly, wondering if he were really serious.

After a moment he went on. "Look, I happen to think that Jesus was one of the world's greatest psychologists. He recognized mental illness as a true disease, back when most people thought it was caused by a curse or a demon. He didn't just heal the blind and the lame, you know—he took on some really serious mental cases and he cured them. To me, God's an important associate in my practice."

It was such a novel idea to Bethany that she could find no words to reply. While Shaun examined the menu, Bethany stared down at the table, thinking about what he had said. She seldom discussed religion with anyone, but she often thought wistfully of the strong faith she'd had as a child, back when her father had still been alive, back before her mother had become so unpredictable—kind one minute, angry and cruel the next.

When the waitress arrived to take their orders, Bethany asked Shaun to select something for her. He chose two cups of black coffee and plates of fruit and cheese. After the waitress had hurried away, Shaun leaned back in his chair and gave Bethany a slow smile. She saw a glint of mischief in his eyes.

"So—have you been wondering about what I said, back there at City Hall?" he asked.

"You know I have," she replied, shaking her head at him in mock reproval. "That's some line, saying I'm the person you've been searching for. Sounds like something out of a second-rate soap opera."

"It does, at that," Shaun agreed, "and, in a way, it is. Bethany, do you know anything about abused children?"

She reeled, feeling as though she'd been struck in the face. "What did you say?"

"Children—abused by their parents. I know you must have read about such things in the paper, or seen it on TV."

She slid her arms off the table and into her lap, clasping the fingers of her right hand about her left wrist. She wanted to get up and run, anywhere, away from those probing eyes. How could he have known? Was he a mind reader?

"I know a little bit about it. Why?" Her voice, forced through a tight throat, rasped harshly.

He pulled a sheet of paper from his jacket pocket,

and she saw he'd saved her sketch of the boy and spaniel.

"Remember when I told you your picture reminded me of a boy I'm trying to help? Bobby looks a lot like this." He laid the picture down on the glass-topped table. "He's a sick little boy. Emotionally, I mean. His father deserted the family a couple of years ago, and his mother now takes her loss out on him. She hurts him, Bethany."

He paused, his brows pulled together, his eyes staring into space as though he were viewing something distressful. Bethany felt grateful that he wasn't looking at her, not at that moment.

He took a deep breath before going on. "We've discovered he has artistic ability." He chuckled, shaking his head. "He draws on *everything*—walls, floors, tables, his bed sheets—with anything he can get his hands on. He has real talent, but obviously needs to be directed. So some of us at the hospital got to thinking—if we could find an artist who'd come to the clinic and work with him—maybe even let him help paint a mural on the cafeteria wall. . . ."

An artist. He'd been looking for an artist.

Bethany felt a stab of disappointment. She realized that she'd been building up a little fantasy in her mind to match the surroundings—that she'd hoped he was going to say she was the girl he'd been dreaming of, his fairy princess come to life, or something equally romantic—and ridiculous.

She cleared her throat. When she spoke, she was relieved to find that her voice sounded normal. "So you thought I might be the one to help you."

He nodded. "Bobby's only nine years old, but he's been through a lot. The last time his mother got drunk, she broke his arm. That's when the authorities brought him to us. He's living at the clinic right now, in a special wing for children with mental or physical problems—kids who can't be returned to their parents just at this time, for one reason or another.'' Now the look on his face was one of appeal. ''So what do you say? Would you be willing to work with him part-time on weekends?''

To give herself time to think, Bethany shifted her chair as though seeking a more comfortable position. Her glance passed over an oval *bas relief* of a Madonna and Child hanging on the east wall of the courtyard in a recessed arch. The expression on the mother's face was serene and kind. The child, leaning against her shoulder, was smiling happily. Bethany stared at the mother's hands, clasping the child in gentle protection. She shivered inside as she remembered how her own mother's hands, caressing one moment, could suddenly slap and pinch . . .

''Bethany, are you there?'' Shaun asked as he waved his fingers in front of her eyes.

''Yes, I was just thinking. . . . Is he—well, violent? If he's been mistreated—''

''No, just withdrawn and very nervous. I mean, if you can't trust your own mother, whom can you trust, right?'' Although he spoke lightly, his face was serious.

She nodded, trying to keep her own expression blank. ''Right.''

She sighed with relief when the waitress arrived with a tray and interrupted the conversation.

''Smells good!'' she said brightly, inhaling the steam from the coffee, which glowed like golden-brown amber through the clear glass cups. The plates

26

were arranged with slices of juicy cantaloupe, plump purple grapes and wedges of cheese. Plucking a grape, Bethany gestured toward the fountain where voluptuous nymphs and naked cherubs offered grapes to the curly-haired Pan. "They'd have to serve grapes here, of course, with figures like that," she went on. "What a contrast between this pagan fountain and that carving of the Madonna. There, on the wall behind you."

Shaun turned and looked toward the maternal grouping. "It would be nice if all mothers were like that, wouldn't it? Unfortunately, they aren't."

Bethany tightened her lips in dismay. She'd hoped to skirt the subject of abused children. Instead, she'd led him right back to it.

"I've already talked with the hospital director about the idea of a mural. This is a state-funded hospital, so we don't have a lot of money for such a project . . . ."

He fixed her again with those blue eyes, and she heard herself saying, "I guess I could donate the time, if you'd furnish the supplies."

His face lit up as though someone had turned on a thousand-watt bulb inside his head. The brilliant flash of his smile sent a swarm of butterflies milling about inside her stomach.

"Great, I was hoping you'd say yes!" he exclaimed. "I'll be going to church in the morning, but I could pick you up tomorrow afternoon, say around two o'clock, and drive you to the hospital to check out the cafeteria wall. Would that be okay?"

She nodded weakly, still in shock that she had agreed to do the mural.

"Just wait'll you meet Bobby," he continued. "He

does have exceptional talent, if we can teach him to control his behavior. I have a hunch you could make the breakthrough with him."

Listening to Shaun rave on about the project, Bethany got a breathless feeling, as though she had indeed fallen from the top of City Hall and was now cartwheeling through space.

Bethany spent the next morning doing her laundry. She'd decided the year before, after the last showdown with her mother, that she'd have to give up church since attending made her feel like a hypocrite. Today she paused, struck with sudden longing, when she heard through her open windows the distant peel of a carillon calling people to worship. Where was Shaun at that moment? she wondered. Perhaps he belonged to the church with the carillon. Perhaps he was already seated in a pew there, dressed in his Sunday best, his hair uncombed—

Although that thought made her smile, she felt the longing for God continue to swell as the bells peeled on.

Lord, she cried, *if You're listening, then You know how confused I am. I want to come back to You, but I just can't, not yet.*

Around one o'clock she showered and dressed, preparing for Shaun's arrival. She rummaged through all her clothes and finally settled for a pink wraparound skirt lined in white and a matching white blouse with pink collar. She brushed her long blond hair until it stood about her shoulders like a soft cloud. After applying a pink gloss to her lips, she then carefully rubbed flesh-colored liquid makeup over the thin network of scars on her left hand and wrist.

Stepping back to survey herself before the mirror in her bedroom, she decided the scars really weren't noticeable unless one were looking for them.

Her early pensive mood had vanished, swallowed up by her excitement at the thought of seeing Shaun again.

Who are you trying to kid? she chided herself. *He doesn't think of you as a woman—you're just an artist who can help him with that boy.*

Nevertheless, when the doorbell rang, she hurried eagerly to let him in, only to stop with a gasp of horror at the sight of him. His left eye was swollen almost shut, while his left cheek sported a purple bruise turning to angry red near his nose.

"Did I do that? Shaun, I'm sorry!"

"Hey, it's okay." A grin spread slowly across his face. He swept one hand up over his forehead, leaving his hair in rumpled disorder. "There's a psychologists' convention in town this week, starting tomorrow, and I'm one of the guest speakers. I'm looking forward to the questions I'm going to get about this eye."

"What will you say?"

"I'll just tell them the truth—that I was decked by a gorgeous girl with a powerful right hook at the top of City Hall!"

"Oh, you! Come on in," she said, stepping aside with a laugh and a wave of her hand.

He entered and swept his gaze around the room. Bethany followed his glance, seeing her own apartment through his eyes—bamboo furniture upholstered in greens and golds, green carpet, pale gold draperies with a delicate leaf pattern, a variety of potted plants resting in or hanging about the room in wicker baskets, books and magazines scattered on the coffee table and, on the walls, her paintings—some realistic, some abstract—products of the different classes she'd taken in school.

Shaun walked over to a surrealistic painting she'd done when she'd been studying the works of Salvadore Dali.

"This is interesting. Weird—but interesting."

She waited nervously while he examined it, afraid that he might try to analyze some of the symbols she'd used. The painting showed a young girl with long blond hair fleeing through a barren landscape. The setting sun, a garish red, was half-concealed by jagged hills on the horizon, looking like a row of snaggled teeth. The girl was barefoot and clothed in a short white tunic. She was being pursued by a figure wearing a hooded black robe. The girl's right arm reached forward, as though for help, toward a twisted leafless tree. From her left shoulder hung not an arm but a shaft of fire, its streaming flames beginning to ignite her dress. On the ground near the tree lay a red rose and a golden key.

Twiddling an imaginary mustache, Shaun turned to her at last and said in a fake German accent, "Vy don't you just lie down on zat couch over zhere and tell ze good doctor all about it?"

"There's nothing much to tell," she said, falling in with his game in spite of herself. She placed the back of her right hand dramatically against her brow and feigned an air of martyrdom. "It's just that I get these headaches . . ."

He dropped the accent and gave her a straightforward look. "No kidding, Bethany, there's a lot of fear in that picture. Is that girl supposed to be you?"

"No, of course not!" she replied emphatically. But she was protesting too strongly, she realized. "Well I suppose there's a little bit of the artist in every painting," she amended, trying to act more casual. "But that's just an exercise I did once for a class. It doesn't mean anything."

"Hmmmm," he said, still holding her with his eyes. She could see he wasn't convinced.

"So how's the weather out there?" she asked brightly, gesturing toward a window. "Do you think it might rain? Should I take a jacket?"

He continued to stare thoughtfully at her for a moment before stepping away from the painting.

"Not a cloud in the sky," he reported and then added, "By the way, may I say you're pretty as a picture yourself today? Wish I were an artist, too, so I could paint your portrait, but I can't even draw a straight line."

She smiled in reply, glad to have recovered a lighter mood. "I can't either, not without a ruler. How often do you see paintings done only with straight lines? Straight lines are boring."

He ran his eyes over her figure. "I agree."

Realizing she'd left herself wide open for that one, she felt a blush warm her face. At the same time, a voice of hope inside whispered that maybe he was attracted to her, after all.

On the way to the hospital Shaun asked her more about her training and background. She explained that she'd graduated from the University of Missouri in Columbia three years before with a degree in art.

"I worked in Columbia as a commercial artist for an

31

advertising firm before being hired by the King Card Company here last fall.''

''And where are you from? Originally, I mean,'' Shaun went on.

She hesitated a moment before answering. ''Oh, just a little town in the Ozarks—Clear Springs, down near the Wild Rivers region. I'm sure you've never heard of it.''

''I went canoeing down there once on the Current River,'' he responded. ''It's pretty country.''

She nodded her agreement. ''Especially right now, with the dogwood in bloom. So . . . what about you, how did you become a psychologist?''

There! She thought triumphantly. *That tosses the ball back in his direction.*

He grinned. ''Someone who's Irish, English and Italian would have to go into psychology just to straighten out his own identity problems, don't you agree? Especially if he's going to be bald by the age of forty. I mean, to face a crisis like that . . .'' He paused dramatically, and she had to laugh.

''You're beautiful when you laugh,'' he told her. ''You should do it more often.''

During the rest of the drive he explained that his English grandmother had been a psychiatric nurse at the Menninger Foundation in Kansas where she met and married a staff psychiatrist of Irish descent. Their only child, a hefty girl with a powerful singing voice, later studied opera in Italy but gave up her career to marry Michael Rosselli, Shaun's father. When they returned to America they opened a restaurant in Kansas City—

''Wait a minute!'' Bethany interrupted. ''You mean *Rosselli's* is your father's place?''

"Best food in town," Shaun stated cheerfully.

"And the woman there who sings opera—"

"—is my Mom," Shaun finished. "I always tell her if she hadn't become a singer, she'd have made a great football player. She's a super lady. We get along well."

Bethany had often heard that a man who got along well with his mother would probably also be good to his wife. Maybe—the thought jolted her back in her seat—maybe he was already married. He wasn't wearing a ring, but that didn't mean much these days.

"How does your wife feel about your work at the hospital?" she asked, fishing.

He shot her a shrewd glance. "No, I'm not married, and no, I'm not dating—anyone special, that is."

Her face burned as she realized she'd betrayed her interest with that question.

She turned her head away, pretending to concentrate on the view through the open window. The road twisted through a wooded area that seemed more rural than suburb. Only an occasional glimpse of a house through the trees told Bethany that they were still inside the city limits.

Shaun turned right into a curving drive that led up through a grove of trees to the gray stone hospital complex sitting on top of a hill. From the parking lot beside the main building, the view opened up, so that Bethany could see the city skyline back toward the west, with the Missouri River sliding along about a mile from the hospital. She watched a long raft being pushed by a river barge and heard a couple of hollow horn blasts echoing faintly through the air.

Shaun began telling her all about his work as he led her inside, so she didn't have to try to talk. Gradually, her embarrassment over her gauche question subsided. After all, she had her answer—the answer she'd hoped to hear.

They walked through several corridors before entering the cafeteria, a large room filled with light. Floor-to-ceiling windows to the north provided a view of the river. To the south, beyond the dining and serving areas, there stretched a long white wall.

Bethany felt a stir of excitement as she ran her eyes over that vast expanse. The fingers of her right hand curled toward the palm and she realized she was clutching an invisible brush. Her arm tingled with anticipation at the thought of loading the brush with thick paint and sweeping over that surface in slick strokes.

She shook her head slightly as she felt a wide grin spread across her face. "Do you know what a challenge that wall presents?"

Shaun chuckled beside her. "I thought it might."

"It'll take a lot of paint," she mused, almost to herself. "Let's see—if we keep the design simple, with large areas for Bobby to fill in . . . kind of like paint-by-the-numbers, to start with . . . hmmm, yes, that would work. And then I could go over it at the end to add the finishing touches . . . I think I see how it could be done. . . ."

Still murmuring to herself, she crossed the cafeteria and ran her fingers over the wall, testing the surface. There was enough bite to it to provide a good base for the paint to cling to, just enough texture to make it interesting. Several men and women, seated about the room at the chrome and formica tables, stared at her in open curiosity, but she didn't mind. Now she felt sure of herself. She was dealing in an area where she had unquestioned authority.

Shaun appeared at her side. "What subject will you choose? Do you have any ideas?"

"Not yet," she replied. "Maybe when I meet Bobby—"

"—which might as well be right now," Shaun finished. "Come along. He's in another building."

Bethany's stomach fluttered at the prospect of facing the child. But Shaun was right; she couldn't put it off.

They left the main building and followed a sidewalk between beds of daffodils to a three-story building set back among some trees. Bethany was shocked to see bars on the first-floor windows and to find the front doors locked. Shaun rang a bell beside the door and it was soon opened by a young guard in a white uniform. After Bethany and Shaun were admitted, the guard relocked the door.

"Is that really necessary?" Bethany asked. "Aren't the patients here just children?"

"Yes, but I told you, some of them are severely disturbed—totally unable to take care of themselves. If a child were to run away . . . Bethany, we've one eight-year-old here who thinks he's from outer space. He no longer speaks English, just some kind of gibberish that only he understands. If we lost him in these woods . . . ."

"Oh," she said in a small voice. For the first time she could sense the difficulties she might encounter in working with Bobby.

But when she met him, her fears vanished. He was a frail child with bright red hair and freckles. His large brown eyes were shadowed by dark circles and his right arm was in a half-cast, from which the ends of his fingers extended like little birds peering from a nest. He was huddled on a couch in the corner of a large bright playroom where several other children were engaged in various activities.

At first glance, the scene looked perfectly normal, like any recreation room filled with children. Only when Bethany had stood there for a moment did she begin to notice evidence of abnormal behavior. One little boy, about five, flung his body back and forth as though he were in an invisible rocking chair. His eyes rolled back slightly in his head while he moaned softly to himself. A girl of about seven twirled past, and Bethany saw plastic diapers under the child's ruffled sundress. Another boy picked up a doll and began trying with dogged determination to tear off its legs. A grandmotherly nurse in a clean white uniform stepped forward and gently took the doll away, saying in a cheerful voice, "John, let's go look out the window and see if there are any boats on the river."

Diverted, the child took the woman's hand. The windows here on the second floor were not barred, but Bethany could see that the panes and screens were both reinforced with heavy mesh.

Shaun led Bethany over to the couch.

"Bobby, I want you to meet Bethany. She's an artist, too." Although Shaun spoke in a soft voice, Bobby still flinched, lifting the cast in front of him like a shield to divert a blow. Bethany felt gall sting her throat. She wanted to take this child in her arms and comfort him.

But she knew she dared not touch him—not yet.

Another attendant, a thin woman of about fifty,

approached and said, "Dr. Rosselli, would you mind stepping over here to the restroom door?"

The tone in her voice implied a hidden meaning behind her request.

Shaun murmured, "Excuse me," and moved away with the woman.

Bethany knelt beside the couch, placing herself on Bobby's level. "Hi, Bobby," she said softly. "I hear you like to draw."

He stared at her with suspicion.

"I like to draw, too," Bethany went on. "Maybe we could draw together. Would you like that?"

He still did not answer but Bethany thought she saw a flicker of interest in his eyes.

"I think we could have a lot of fun, and maybe we could get to be friends," she continued. "That would be neat. It's fun to have friends."

I sound like a fool, she thought. *Children pick up on that.*

She searched frantically for a different approach. Before she could begin, however, Shaun called, "Beth, come over here for a minute. I want you to see something."

Bethany gave Bobby a reassuring wink. "I'll be right back."

When she joined Shaun, she heard the attendant saying worriedly, "I'm really sorry, Dr. Rosselli. I don't know where he got that felt tip pen. We've been so careful—"

Shaun gave Bethany a little bow while gesturing toward the restroom. She stepped up to the door and gasped. Scrawled across the wall next to the sink was a huge green horse with flowing mane and tail. Its neck was arched, its nostrils flared.

"Bobby's latest," Shaun told her. "What do you think?"

She shook her head in awe. "I think it's incredible. Shaun, that kid's got real talent."

Shaun laughed, a brief burst filled both with admiration and chagrin. "We think so, too. But what we have to do is teach him how to use his talent in constructive ways. Are you still willing to give it a go?"

"More than ever," she replied. "But how does he do it, with that cast on his arm?"

"Just our luck—he happens to be left-handed." Again, Shaun's voice held mixed emotions.

"We haven't found where he hid the pen yet. Oh, no! There he goes again!" cried the attendant.

Bethany and Shaun whipped about to see Bobby down on the floor. His left hand, clutching a pen, scrabbled frantically over the tiles in wide, sweeping strokes. It was obvious he knew he had to finish before they stopped him. When they hurried across the room, he dropped to the floor and curled up in a ball, as though presenting his back for blows. Before him on the tan tiles was the hastily scrawled outline of a dog with floppy ears and a long tail.

Shaun knelt and gently touched the boy's shoulder. "It's all right, Bobby. We're not going to hit you."

Bethany knelt, too. "That's a beautiful dog, Bobby. I think his name is Rover."

Bobby turned his head and opened one eye. "No," he announced in a husky little voice. "His name is Bad Boy."

"Bad Boy?" Bethany repeated, somewhat taken aback. "That's a strange name for a—"

Shaun interrupted, speaking to the child in a soft

but firm tone: "The dog you drew is not a "bad boy,"
and you're not a bad boy, either. You're a good artist,
and you and Bethany are going to paint a picture
together in the cafeteria where all the visitors who
come here can see it."

Bethany mentally kicked herself for not having
recognized the guilt the boy had revealed in the name
he'd given the dog. She, of all people, should have
known how little self-esteem Bobby would have,
living with a mother who undoubtedly kept telling him
he was a 'bad boy' to justify the punishment she was
giving him. Bethany remembered the nights she had
cried herself to sleep, not because of the pain in her
body from her mother's blows, but because of the
pain in her spirit from her mother's wounding words:
"You're a bad girl, Bethany. Bad. I don't like you
when you're bad."

She returned to the present to hear Shaun continue,
"We're going to let you paint on a wall, Bobby, with
lots of colors and big brushes. Bethany will paint with
you. But meanwhile, do us a favor, okay? Draw on
the paper we give you, not in the restrooms or on the
floor."

Bobby scooted away and planted himself with his
back against the wall. He stared, owl-eyed, at Shaun
and Bethany with his mouth clenched tight. But
Bethany could see intelligence behind the boy's wary
expression. She knew he had heard. Looking at those
freckles and that mop of red hair, she suddenly had a
vision of Bobby in patched overalls and a battered
straw hat.

"Huckleberry Finn," she murmured aloud.

Shaun glanced at her with one eyebrow raised.
"What?"

39

"I think I know what the mural will be," she said, watching the images take shape in her mind. "A river scene, mirroring the view of the river from those windows in the cafeteria, with Huckleberry Finn and Tom Sawyer on a raft. I'll use Bobby as the model for Huck Finn. And we can even put a horse and a dog in the picture, maybe running along the shore—"

"That's a great idea!" Shaun interrupted enthusiastically. "Bobby would really get into that. Beth, I know this is going to work out well."

He threw his arms around her in a spontaneous hug, which turned her knees to melted butter. She hoped, more fervently than she had hoped for anything else in her life, that she wouldn't let him down.

CHAPTER 3

BETHANY HUMMED HAPPILY the next morning as she dressed for work, remembering Shaun's hug at the hospital and the pleasant chat they'd had later during the drive when he brought her home. He hadn't taken her to dinner, but had asked for a "rain check," explaining that he needed to go home and work on his talk for the psychologists' convention.

"But the conference ends on Friday, and I'll be ready for a break by then," he'd said. "How about going to dinner with me that night at my folks' place? You might come up with some new questions about the mural, and we can talk about them."

She'd agreed at once, happy that he wanted to see her again.

Now she turned before the mirror, checking to make sure that everything was properly fastened on her yellow dress and its matching jacket. A shaft of sunlight streaming through her bedroom window caught in the edges of her hair, creating a golden halo about her head. Her dress glowed as brightly as if its threads were made of individual sunbeams.

She continued to hum while fixing a small pot of coffee and a poached egg on toast for breakfast. Later, as she maneuvered her compact car through the morning rush-hour traffic, she shook her head in amazement at the turn her life had taken. In just two days, she had moved from "famine" to "feast," from the depression of loneliness to involvement with an intriguing man *and* the start of a challenging project.

Challenging, indeed. Bobby's freckled face rose before her in her mind's eye, and she felt her heart turn over with sympathy. She continued to think about him during the drive to work, was still thinking about him when she reached her special cubicle in the large artists' workshop at the King Card Company. Once there, however, her attention turned to the work at hand. She had a presentation due for critique the next day and she still wasn't satisfied with her illustrations.

Switching on the fluorescent light above her drawing table, she lifted away the large sheet of cardboard covering her work from the preceding Friday. She perched on the stool and leaned forward to reread the latest sympathy verse she'd been given to illustrate:

There's little we can say or do
To soothe the grief you bear,
But ask the Lord to keep you
In His wise and loving care.
We pray His strength to guide you,
Supporting in all ways,
As He walks along beside you
Throughout the coming days.

Bethany chewed her lower lip as she thoughtfully examined the drawing she'd made the week before of a gate opening onto a garden filled with flowers. She put it to one side and took a fresh sheet of paper. Quickly she sketched one long-stemmed rose lying on a table beside an open Bible, then added a lighted candle in a slender candlestick. After enclosing the sketch in an oval frame, she scripted the words: *May God Be With You*.

She sat back to view the sketch with a critical eye. It wasn't overwhelmingly original, yet there was something soothing about it.

If the cover were double-layered . . .

The idea grew in her mind, step by step. She envisioned the outer layer in a rich cream color with both the oval frame and the blessing, *May God Be With You*, embossed in gold. The center of the frame would be die cut, revealing the picture of the Bible, the rose and the candle printed on pale gold foil and glowing with light. The verse would be printed inside, using a delicate old-fashioned script.

Somewhat predictable, yet she felt it would appeal to those who wanted something a little warmer and more personal than the formal silver-on-white that was so often used.

She decided to work up the concept to present to the committee, along with the sketch of the gate and garden, as well as a third idea that featured the words, *May God Be With You*, in blue-gray at the bottom of a white card. The scene painted in delicate pastels included a path in the foreground, curving back toward distant hills where rays of the setting sun fanned upward to touch layered clouds and one soaring bird.

She worked hard all morning, skipping her usual coffee break. When she straightened at last and looked at the small clock sitting on the shelf beside her drawing table, she couldn't believe how fast the time had gone. She stretched her cramped shoulders and then slid off the stool.

Clam chowder, that's what I want for lunch, she decided. *Plus a tossed salad with ranch-style dressing and iced tea. Maybe even peach pie for dessert. No, wait a minute. . . .* She paused, smiling as she thought of Shaun. *Make that butter pecan ice cream.*

Bethany left the King Card Company building and crossed a courtyard to enter the multi-leveled Crown Center shopping complex. As she tread the carpeted corridors, she inhaled with pleasure the spicy scent wafting from a soap and candle shop. Caught up in the aura of the colorful center, she peered through open doorways at toys, books, antiques, jewelry, clothing, flowers, stained glass and other treasures beautifully displayed to tempt even the most reluctant shopper.

Coming out at last on the second level overlooking the main lobby, she paused to admire the rainbow-hued banners suspended from the ceiling, then glanced through the two-story-high glass walls toward a small park where fountains splashed, slender columns of water lined up like soldiers before an abstract sculpture in orange metal . . . .

She went weak in the knees at the sight of Shaun striding up the walk and through the tall glass doors into the lobby below. He was impeccably dressed in a tailored suit with matching vest and tie, his hair neatly combed for a change, his polished leather shoes twinkling as he marched purposefully along. With briefcase in hand, he looked quite the professional businessman—except for his swollen cheek and black eye.

Bethany took a deep breath to slow her pounding heart, then called, "Shaun!", hoping to attract his attention before he disappeared beneath the balcony.

She hurried onto the escalator, stumbling in her haste, and grabbed the railing for support as the treads carried her downward. He spotted her and smiled in sudden recognition.

"Bethany!"

Shaun met her at the foot of the escalator and held out a hand to steady her when she stepped off. Her arm tingled at his touch.

"You're a sight for sore eyes," he joked.

She grimaced, reaching a tentative hand to touch his bruised cheek. "I really am sorry about that. Has anyone noticed?"

He threw back his head in a burst of hearty laughter. "Has anyone noticed?! I'm the hero of the hour. This eye gives me a charisma I've never known before—my friends look at me askance, imagining all kinds of dark and dramatic secrets in my background. When I gave my speech at the conference this morning, there wasn't an empty seat in the house."

"Then your speech is over? How did it go?"

"Just fine, thanks to the work I did on it last night. Are you on your lunch break?"

"Yes."

"Me, too. I have to serve on a panel this afternoon, so I slipped away to be by myself and go over some notes. Hadn't expected to run into you! Those notes can wait. Is it okay if I join you, instead?"

The smile he beamed down upon her was so

intimate that the lobby seemed to vanish before Bethany's eyes, leaving the two of them alone. Then the illusion faded and she was back in the real world once more, reminding herself that this man saw her merely as a person he'd contracted to help him with his work—nothing more. Nevertheless, the prospect of being with him for this hour seemed like a gift from heaven.

"All right, where shall we sit?"

She turned to survey the small round tables and bentwood chairs nestled among potted trees in the lobby, producing ambience of an outdoor Parisian café.

"I've got an idea!" Shaun suddenly said, his eyes lighting with blue flame. "Let's get sandwiches and go eat them by the waterfall in the Crown Center Hotel."

Which was, in Bethany's estimation, the second most romantic spot in the city, next to the Country Club Plaza. The architects, in designing the hotel, had used, as one wall of the lobby, a natural hillside, complete with rocks, waterfall and trees. Bethany had often yearned to climb the metal walkway with a man who would hold her hand and profess his love, there among the flowers that rioted in bright profusion along the rocky ledges. At least today she could sit by the falls and pretend that her dream was coming true, even if she knew it was just that—a dream. Shaun turned then to read the menu posted above a nearby food counter, accidentally brushing against Bethany's arm. She gasped at the contact and could feel her pulse accelerate.

This won't do! she told herself in dismay. *You've got to control yourself, my girl!*

But she wasn't sure she could, not beside a singing

46

waterfall surrounded by flowers—and not with Shaun Rosselli, who was, she admitted at last, the most attractive man she'd ever met.

"The turkey sandwiches here are good," Shaun commented, bringing her back to earth. "Would you like coffee or iced tea?"

"Tea, please," she replied, surprised but pleased that she could speak in such a normal tone.

Shaun set down his briefcase and stepped to the counter where he placed the order, soon returning with a cardboard tray containing two plastic-wrapped sandwiches and tea in large paper cups. She picked up his briefcase, and they walked together along a carpeted corridor and down the steps into the lobby of the hotel. The splashing of the waterfall, echoing off to the left through a wide passageway, filled Bethany with excited anticipation, the same feeling she sometimes got when leaving on a vacation. Her breath quickened as she and Shaun stepped from the wood-paneled lobby into the scented moist air of the three-story high room with its frosted glass ceiling. Light filtered through leaf lace to throw gleaming reflections over the falls that cascaded like silver hair down the dark rocks into the sparkling pool below. Pots of purple orchids nestled among natural ferns on the cliffside, adding to the illusion of a tropical paradise.

They proceeded to the balcony overlooking the pool where they sat together on a bench. Shaun carefully placed the tray of food between them. He unwrapped his sandwich at once and ate with gusto. On the contrary, Bethany found that her appetite had fled. She nibbled at her sandwich, remembering having read somewhere that falling in love can take away the desire for food. Well, if that was the test, then she just might be in love with Shaun Rosselli, but he most assuredly was not in love with *her!*

After washing down a bite of sandwich with a big swallow of tea, Shaun asked, "How's the card business going?"

Bethany shrugged. "I'm still working on sympathy cards. I wish my supervisor would let me design birthday cards for a change—the kind of card where I could paint children and dogs, like the sketch you looked at on Saturday."

He grinned. "I've got that sketch pinned on my kitchen wall. Hope that's okay with you . . . that I kept it, I mean. Although that really isn't fair, I should have offered to buy it . . . "

"Oh, no!" Bethany protested. "I'm flattered that you want it. But it's torn. I wish you had something better . . . "

"For me, there couldn't be a drawing I like better. This one is special."

For a moment Bethany dared hope that it was special to him because of her. Then she realized it was because the drawing looked like Bobby. She gave herself another mental shake. You've got to *stop fantasizing, Bethany.*

"By the way, I phoned a member of the hospital board this morning before leaving home and told him I'd found the artist to work on the mural," he now told her. "He said that the board would like to see some sketches first, and a list of your credentials. I guess they didn't feel they could take my word that you're the right person for the job. Hospital policy. I hope you understand . . . "

"Yes, of course," she replied briskly. But her heart sank like a stone cast into a pool. What if the board turned her down? That would mean the end of her association with Shaun. She hadn't realized until that moment just how much she'd been looking forward to working with him on the project, despite her concern that he might try to probe too deeply into the secret corners of her mind.

"When does the committee want to see the sketches?" she went on, striving for a businesslike tone.

"As soon as you can work them up. Would it be possible to come up with something by the end of the week—maybe some rough drafts by Saturday? We're having a special board meeting that morning to talk about a couple of other issues. It would be good if I could show them something then. Or am I pushing you too much? Since I'm not an artist, I don't know just how much work the sketches will take."

Bethany chewed her lower lip, pondering it. Such a tight schedule would indeed present problems. She'd have to work at home every night that week, laying out different ideas and trying to come up with a simplified approach that would challenge Bobby without frustrating him. Of course, she didn't have any other plans for the week, at least not until Friday night when she was supposed to have dinner at *Rosselli's* with Shaun.

"I could try," she said at last, "but I really do want the sketches to be good, and they may not turn out right if I rush. Maybe you can look at them Friday night, when you come to pick me up, and tell me then if you approve."

"Oh, good, you *are* still going out with me," he said, raking his hand through his hair so that it stood in wild shocks on top of his head. "I was hoping you hadn't changed your mind!"

She stared for a brief moment at the picture he now presented—sharp business suit, tousled hair and black eye—and she felt laughter rise like a warm lump of dough, yeasty and light, expanding until she could contain it no longer.

"Shaun, I'm sorry, but you look so funny, like a little boy who dressed up for church and then got into a fight with the neighborhood bully. Do you have a comb in your pocket?"

He grinned, fishing around until he found a small black comb that he handed to her with a bow.

"See what you can do, okay? I can't look *too* bad at the conference, or my reputation really will be shot!"

She rose and ran the comb through his rebellious black locks before trying to pat them into place. The touch of his hair, a feathery kiss against her palms, sent shivers of pleasure up her arms. At the same time she felt a tenderness toward him for the trust he displayed in allowing her to perform this personal task. She didn't want to stop, but knew that any more time spent in such an activity might reveal the depth of her emotions.

"There," she said, handing him the comb. "All done."

"When I'm bald, this will no longer be a problem," he replied cheerfully.

"I think you made that up—about being bald someday," she told him, placing her fists on her hips to look at him sternly. "At the age of ninety, you'll be running around with snow-white hair sticking out all over your head, looking like those pictures of Dr. Einstein."

"That's some future you're painting for me," he said, laughing.

The future—a blank page ready for any illustration she chose to put there. She continued to eye him speculatively as she mentally sketched a picture—of the future. Shaun in a chair before a fire, bald head glinting in the flames; herself seated in a rocker on the other side, sketch book in hand; and her paintings hanging on the walls. A little boy sat to one side building a tower out of Tinker Toys—a boy with red hair and freckles . . .

"Bethany? What's the matter?"

Shaun's voice broke her reverie.

"Oh, nothing, I was just checking to make sure your hair was really okay," she said as she strolled back to the bench and resumed her seat. To cover her confusion, she picked up her sandwich and took another bite, but the food tasted like cardboard on her tongue.

Shaun swallowed another drink of tea, then absently wiped his mouth with a paper napkin. "I keep thinking about the mural," he said. "I can't tell you what it's going to mean to Bobby to work on that with you."

"I keep thinking about him, too. That look in his eyes—so frightened, and yet you can tell he's very intelligent." Other questions came flooding back—questions that had haunted her ever since she'd met the child. "There's—there's something else that's bothered me all weekend," she finally said. "For innocent children to be hurt like that . . . you said in Chandler Court that God understands the children's problems, that He helps you in your work. Well, if

He's such a loving God, how can He let children be abused in the first place?"

The minute the words were out, she regretted having spoken them. Shaun was obviously a firm believer, a man with no doubts about God's actions. What must he be thinking of her?

Shaun looked at her thoughtfully for a long moment. Then he said, "Free will. God gives us free will."

"To harm a child? No, I can't accept that!" In her agitation she flung out one hand and accidentally knocked over her tea. Ice splattered across the concrete floor of the balcony like broken glass. She rose at once, her face burning, and hastened to gather up the ice and put it back in her empty cup. She mopped up the spill with a napkin, then flung the refuse into a nearby trash basket. She glanced sideways to see Shaun still regarding her with narrowed eyes.

But when he finally spoke, there was no condemnation in his voice. "There are times when I wonder about it, too, of course, when a child who's been battered is admitted to the hospital. That's certainly not how God wants parents to behave. He wants us to be loving and kind. But evil behavior in mankind does *not* come from God, Bethany. Surely you know that. There are other influences here on earth, evil influences . . ."

"Yes, I do know that," she interrupted impatiently. "Still, God *could* intervene, once in a while, to keep children from being harmed. That's all I'm asking—"

"And He could stop traffic accidents and fires and wars and crime and turn the world back into a Garden of Eden—a peaceful, beautiful place like this," Shaun replied, waving his hand toward the waterfall. "He could do it all for us, Bethany, make our lives absolutely perfect. But how could we learn, then. How could we grow? Sometimes a loving parent has to let his children make mistakes—"

"Okay, I see your point. You're saying that God is a loving Father who gives us free will, the right to make mistakes and learn from them. All right, I'll go along with that—so long as it applies to adults. But I'll bet you, Shaun, if you walked in on Bobby's mother beating him, you wouldn't stand back and argue 'free will.' You'd *stop* her—by force, if necessary!"

She realized then that she'd lifted her voice. She stood in shock as the echoes of her words bounced off the cliff-face opposite the balcony. Several people who were climbing the stairs through the treetops paused to glance in her direction. She struggled for control, furious with herself for having gotten into such an argument in the first place.

Shaun came to stand before her, reaching out to hold both her arms while he studied her face.

"Who hurt you, Bethany?" he asked quietly. "Who hurt you so much?"

She hung her head to avoid looking into those intense eyes, now earnest with concern. She swallowed hard, determined not to cry. Stepping back, she pulled free from his grip.

"I'm just thinking about the kids in the hospital, that's all." She took a few steps to stand by the balcony railing. "I'm all right now. Let's talk about something else, okay?"

When she turned back to him, she managed a bright smile but she felt that she hadn't fooled him one bit.

His eyes were indeed searchlights, probing the very recesses of her soul. He nodded slightly as though he knew she could no longer bear to pursue the subject.

"I really have to get back to the conference," he said, glancing at his watch. "Come on, I'll walk with you as far as the escalator."

Bethany felt deflated, and angry with herself for having spoiled the romantic mood of this place. She wished she could erase the last five minutes, return to the moment just before that—the easy banter, the warm companionship. But it was too late now. The damage was done. She walked beside him without saying more back through the hotel and into the shopping center. They passed a seashell shop, glowing like Poseidon's jeweled grotto.

Suddenly Shaun took her arm and turned her around, leading her into the shop. "Do you mind if we stop in here for just a moment? There's something I want to look for," he said as he disengaged her arm and strode off to speak with a clerk.

As she waited, Bethany wandered down one of the aisles, feeling her ruffled emotions smooth under the spell of the beautiful displays. Fans of rosy coral seemed to wait for the grip of a mermaid's hand, while giant conches curled rough lips back from silky peach-colored mouths to roar the call of the sea. She paused beside a sculpture of a leaping dolphin supported by an almost invisible wire above a rolling wave carved from turquoise. She'd always been fascinated by dolphins. She'd read that dolphins were conscientious parents, very protective of their young. She realized she'd never heard of dolphin, or a whale, for that matter, ever indulging in "child abuse."

Shaun came up to her then and handed her a pale

blue paper bag stamped with pictures of seashells in white.

"Bought you a little present," he said.

She opened the bag to draw forth a round white shell and a postcard. The card bore a picture of the shell, along with the words, THE LEGEND OF THE SAND DOLLAR, followed by a story printed in blue script.

"Read it," Shaun urged.

Quickly Bethany scanned the lines: *The sand dollar is a very unusual shell. The five slits around the edge represent the five wounds in the body of Christ—the nail holes in His hand and feet, and the cut in His side made by the thrust of the Roman spear. On the top of the shell is an Easter lily, with the five-pointed Star of Bethlehem in the center. On the back is the outline of a Poinsettia, the Christmas flower. Break open the shell and you will release five small white doves, messengers from God, to spread Good Will and Peace to all Mankind.*

"It's a lovely story," she told Shaun as she cradled the sand dollar in her hand. "Thank you."

He nodded. "I've always liked that little legend. Carry the shell in your purse . . . a kind of keepsake from me. Maybe sometime when you're feeling down, it will remind you of God's love and make you feel better. And, Bethany, please remember, I'm your friend. If you ever need to talk, call me, okay?"

Bethany's throat tightened with unshed tears. She carefully wrapped the fragile shell in the blue bag and then put it, along with the card, in a zippered side pocket in her purse for safekeeping. She knew that she would keep the shell always, a reminder of this day and this man, even though she suspected that he would soon forget her after she and Bobby finished the mural.

When they reached the top of the escalator, Shaun said, "Well, I've got to go now. See you Friday night."

Before she realized what he was doing, Shaun snatched up her left hand and planted a quick kiss on the back. She felt him flinch, saw him lift his head to peer with a puzzled frown at the scars there. Her heart thudded in panic. She grabbed her hand away and lowered it to her side, concealing it in the folds of her skirt.

"I'll get to work on those sketches tonight," she said evenly.

Shaun held her eyes for one brief moment, a searching look that she chose to ignore. Finally he turned and rode the escalator down to the lobby, then hurried away, stopping to give her a quick wave before pushing out through the doors. She watched him go, her emotions tumbling as wildly as the splashing water in the fountain outside.

Listen, God, out of all the men You could have sent in answer to my prayer, did it have to be a psychologist who works with abused children? she called silently, wondering if God might possibly have a strange sense of humor. Was it sacrilegious to think such a thing? Or did He have a plan in all this?

CHAPTER 4

BETHANY'S HEART BEAT FASTER in anticipation of Shaun's arrival as she spread out her sketches on the dining table and kitchen counter. She'd worked hard on them every night—drawing, discarding, trying again, as she pulled together scenes from Mark Twain's beloved novels.

Bobby's freckled face, now the model for Huckleberry Finn, peered out to her from page after page. In one scene he lounged on the grass patting a dog, his uncombed hair jutting from beneath a tattered straw hat, while several other boys slapped whitewash on a board fence. In another scene he poled a raft through swirling muddy water, his overalls' legs rolled up to his knees, his bare feet planted firmly on the logs. Tom Sawyer, in white shirt and black knickers, with black curly hair blowing in the wind, reknotted one corner of a red bandanna handkerchief that fluttered, a defiant flag, from a stripped sapling pole toward the rear of the raft.

Bethany's breath caught in a quick gasp as she took a second look at her Tom Sawyer. She'd thought she was just making him up, a composite of various children she had known. Now she realized that her subconscious, a capricious trickster, had done it again. If she took twenty years away from Shaun Churchill Rosselli and dressed him in knickers, there he'd be, the "spittin' image" of the Tom in her picture.

The doorbell chimed, sending her pulse skittering like a startled rabbit. Would Shaun recognize himself in these pictures? Warmth suffused her face. She stepped quickly to a mirror for a last check of her bell sleeved white silk blouse and softly gathered gold wool skirt. The flush had spread to her cheeks, giving her a pulsing glow of health while emphasizing the sparkle in her gold-and-green eyes. She briefly touched the gold chain about her throat and felt it quiver with the throbbing of her pulse.

When she opened the door she saw that, during the four-day interval since she'd met Shaun at Crown Plaza, the swelling about his eye had subsided, leaving the bruise on his cheek a strange shade of green instead of its original angry purple. Now he lounged nonchalantly against the door jamb, his broad shoulders bulging beneath the gray tweed of his sports coat. His charcoal gray slacks fit neatly over his trim hips while his shirt lay casually open at the collar. Instead of a tie he wore once more on its strong chain the silver cross, gleaming brightly against the expanse of his chest. But it was his hair that caught Bethany's attention. The black curls sprang wildly about his forehead as though he'd been caught in a high wind. When he saw the direction of Bethany's gaze, he lifted one hand and quickly tried to correct the errant locks, but without success.

She felt a grin spread across her face at the boyish gesture. He grinned, too, meeting her laughing eyes with a flash that electrified her. Warmth sparked across the space between them, an arc of almost visible light. Bethany gulped, trying to regain her composure. She'd never met a man who could affect her this way, a man whose gaze was like a physical touch.

"Co—come on in," she stammered. "I have something to show you."

She whirled and led the way back into the living room where the drawings were spread out over all available surfaces like a fall of very large and brightly colored leaves.

Shaun let out an appreciative whistle. "You *have* been busy."

He walked slowly around the dining table, pausing here and there to examine a sketch more closely. At last he picked up the one of the two boys on a raft.

"Looks just like him!" he exclaimed in delight.

For a moment Bethany feared he had spotted his own likeness in the figure of Tom Sawyer but, as she watched, he tapped the drawing of Huck Finn with his finger.

"How did you manage to capture that expression without his being here to pose?" he went on. "These are wonderful!"

Pleasure pulsed through Bethany at his praise. "Do you think the board will approve?"

"If they don't they should have their heads examined."

He laughed at his own joke and Bethany joined him,

picturing a fleet of stern-faced board members laid out in rows on black leather couches, ready for analysis. She had a vision of Shaun holding a notebook while asking sternly, "And just what happened in your childhood that makes you now resent Huckleberry Finn?"

"How is Bobby?" she asked aloud. "Any change in his condition since last weekend?"

Shaun shook his head. "Just about the same. I include him in my prayers every day. I hope you do, too."

Bethany shifted her shoulders with sudden discomfort. Shaun spoke of prayer in such a matter-of-fact way, as though it were something he took for granted she would do. Again she felt like a hypocrite, standing there with doubt in her heart. Did he really think that prayer could make a difference in the life of a disturbed child? Analysis she could accept as being of some help, and the positive effort of working on the mural might indeed have therapeutic value. But prayer to an unseen God who might not even be listening—well, she just didn't know.

Her own prayers, muttered at odd intervals throughout each day, seemed to drift upward into some dark void and get lost along with way. She'd never had actual proof that any of them had ever been answered, unless she counted that prayer on top of City Hall when she had asked God to send her someone to love. Shaun's appearance at that moment had seemed somewhat like a "God send," and yet, if she stopped to think about it rationally, she had to admit that the whole thing could have been coincidence.

She came back with a start as Shaun snapped his fingers in front of her eyes.

"Hey, are you there?" he asked. "You look like you're a million miles away."

"Sorry, I was just thinking about the mural. I'm anxious to get started on it."

"You can't be any more anxious to begin than I am to have you do so. I really expect great things from this project, Bethany. Listen, let's leave the sketches here for now, and I'll pick them up when I bring you home this evening. That way, you'll have to invite me in to say good night!"

The smile he gave her was guileless, yet he managed to convey just a tiny hint of lechery under his words, like a boy—again, she thought of Tom Sawyer—playing at being seductive. He looked so adorable that Bethany had to laugh.

"Your whole face lights up when you laugh," Shaun said, eyeing her with obvious approval. "You have a slight dimple, did you know that? Right there . . ."

He reached out and touched her left cheek with one fingertip. The caress, as delicate as the touch of a feather, sent shivers racing down her back. She looked into his amazing blue eyes, stained glass glowing with inner light, and felt again the melting sensation in her arms and legs that always left her breathless. She thought for one brief moment that he was going to kiss her, and her lips parted slightly on a barely suppressed gasp of anticipation. However, he took his hand away from her face while saying cheerfully, "Well, we'd better get started. I told my Dad to make our reservation for six-thirty."

She lowered her eyes to hide the emotions that

assailed her. She wanted him to caress her face again with that gentle touch that was so different from anything she'd ever experienced before. Yes, he was physically attractive, that she couldn't deny nor did she wish to; but she realized that it was also his gentle humor, his genuine kindness, which moved her in this strange way, evoking responses she hadn't known were possible. She'd always considered herself a lady—on the restrained side, at that. But now she felt her heart stir within her, a flower opening to the light.

Get hold of yourself, she admonished herself fiercely. *He's not in love with you. He sees you as an artist, that's all. He's made that clear from the start.*

Then why couldn't she control her reaction to him? Why did her knees tremble whenever he came near?

"All right, I'm ready," she announced, pleased that her voice did not betray her feelings.

In the car she asked him about his day and then settled down in one corner of the seat, composing herself further for the upcoming encounter with his parents while letting his voice wash over her in a soothing flow.

When they reached the restaurant, even though she'd been there a couple of times before, she examined the outside of the building with new interest, seeing it now as a part of Shaun's life and background. With white stuccoed facade and red-tiled roof, lacy wrought iron gates, and a three-tiered fountain splashing merrily in the middle of a flower-filled courtyard, the restaurant reminded Bethany of pictures she'd seen in books about the Mediterranean. She eagerly walked with Shaun through the garden and into the lobby. There, she was assailed by a riot of red—polished red tile floor, embossed wallpaper in red and gold, benches covered in red leather. A chandelier with glassblown fruit and golden leaves glittered overhead, its light reflected in mirrors set into niches along the walls.

"Shaun!"

Bethany turned at the sound of a deep, hearty voice to see a large woman bearing down upon them with her arms outstretched. The woman's dark hair was swept up dramatically on top of her head and held in place by a glittering tiara. She wore a flowing, low-cut ball gown in pale blue silk that shimmered through the delicate lace of a floor-length redingote. Against the creamy skin of her ample bosom there sparkled a necklace that matched the tiara.

"Papa, look it's Shaun!"

A man in a black tuxedo and ruffled white shirt now appeared from an archway leading into the dining area. Although he was shorter than either his wife or son, there was a strength about him that made itself felt at once. His gleaming bald head reflected the lights of the chandelier.

Shaun glanced toward Bethany, flashing her an amused smile, which she returned. She felt very close to Shaun at that moment as they shared the private joke about his father's baldness.

After hugging both his parents, Shaun announced, "This is Bethany Clark, the girl who blacked my eye."

Bethany wanted to fall through the floor with embarrassment, but Shaun's parents appeared unabashed.

"What did he do to you, poor girl, that you had to hit him?" asked his mother as she gave her son a stern look that Bethany could see was a put-on. It was obvious she adored him.

"I threatened her honor on top of City Hall, and she had to defend herself," Shaun replied.

"That's my son," said his father, patting him on the shoulder. "Truly a hot-blooded Italian."

The love and warmth between Shaun and his parents filled Bethany with amazement. And envy. Never had she felt a rapport like that with her own mother. What might her childhood have been like, she wondered, if she and her mother could have been friends . . .

"Right this way," Mr. Rosselli was saying. "I've reserved the best table in the house for you, *bella donna*—my beautiful lady." With an elaborate bow, he took Bethany's arm and led her toward the dining room. "As for this beast of a son, I should make him eat out in the alley."

Bethany flung an amused look back over her shoulder toward Shaun, who just grinned as he followed behind with his mother. They proceeded to a table in the front of the dining room near a small stage with a baby grand piano. Mr. Rosselli pulled out a chair upholstered in red velvet for Bethany and gallantly seated her. She touched the smooth surface of the gleaming white brocade tablecloth with her fingertips while inhaling the scent of fresh roses nodding in a silver vase. Shaun seated his mother and then took the chair opposite Bethany.

"I would stay to protect you from my son, but there is a minor problem in the kitchen to which I must attend," Mr. Rosselli said to Bethany with a friendly smile.

Shaun reacted with a look of dismay, which did not

disguise the underlying mischief. "Since I've told Bethany you serve the best food in town, I hope you and the chef can work things out. I wouldn't want your reputation damaged."

"You can sit there with that black eye and worry about *my* performance?" his father remonstrated. "But do not fear! Everything will soon be under control."

Mr. Rosselli bowed to his wife and then kissed his fingertips toward Bethany before bustling away. Bethany smiled at Shaun and nodded slightly to show that she liked his father. Shaun smiled back, returning her nod. From the corner of her eye, Bethany saw Mrs. Rosselli glance with eager attention toward them both as though she wondered exactly what their relationship might be. If his mother were actually to ask the question aloud, what would be Shaun's reply, Bethany wondered. Employer and employee? Just friends?

A slim young man dressed in black tails and carrying an arm load of music came out onto the stage and seated himself at the piano. As he shuffled the music about on the rack, obviously attempting to arrange it in a particular order, he called out to Mrs. Rosselli, "We are doing the aria from *The Barber of Seville* first tonight, aren't we?"

"No, I think I'll start with the *Carmen* medley." The older woman turned toward Bethany and gave her a quizzical look. "Unless you have a particular request?"

Not wanting to admit that she knew very little about opera, Bethany said, "Anything you sing will be fine with me."

"Well, Mom, *I* think you should specialize in

Wagner," Shaun stated innocently, but Bethany caught a teasing glint in his eyes. "I can just see you in a Valkyrie costume, with the shield—"

"And the horned helmet?" Mrs. Rosselli interrupted, finishing the statement for him. "That would take away the customers' appetites for sure!"

Bethany and Shaun joined in her laughter. There was something warm and genuine about the woman that Bethany already admired, even on such short acquaintance.

"Musical talent always amazes me," Bethany now commented. "I can't even carry a tune."

Shaun reached out to touch her hand. The contact electrified her and she felt the telltale flush once more sweep from her neck and up into her face. She lowered her head, trying to hide her reaction, while Shaun, seemingly unaware of her predicament, countered her statement. "But she's an excellent artist, Mom. She's going to paint a mural for us at the hospital."

"Maybe," Bethany put in quickly. "Shaun, you forget, the board hasn't approved me yet."

"They will," he replied emphatically. "If they don't . . ."

" . . . they should have their heads examined," she finished in unison with him.

"Right."

Mr. Rosselli came bustling back, a big smile on his face. "Everything is settled with the chef," he announced. "I have taken the liberty of ordering the speciality of the house for our dinner tonight—*Veal Parmigiano*. I hope you'll like it . . ."

"She will," Shaun assured his father. "Just wait until you taste it, Bethany," he continued enthusiastically. "My Dad has worked out his own combination of spices . . . "

Mrs. Rosselli rolled her eyes heavenward. "I'd better start singing now, while I still have some voice left. After a big meal I always sing flat, and that really *could* scare the customers away!"

She rose and swept majestically to the stage. There was instant applause from the diners scattered about the room. After a few words of welcome to the audience, Mrs. Rosselli nodded to the pianist to begin the introduction. He launched into a rousing Spanish melody that sounded familiar to Bethany.

"The *Habañera*, from *Carmen*," Shaun whispered.

And then Mrs. Rosselli began to sing, in a messo-soprano so rich and full that it flowed over the room like an incoming ocean tide. Bethany felt the hairs lift on her arm in a chill of pleasure at the beauty of the sound. She slid a quick glance toward Shaun and saw his eyes shining with pride as he listened to his mother. Mr. Rosselli's beaming face resembled the rising sun. Her family was obviously devoted to her, Bethany thought.

The woman's eyes flashed and she swayed with subtle flirtatiousness, glancing toward her husband while singing in English:

Love's a bird so free and wild,
A bird that one can never tame.
In vain is all your wooing mild
If he refuse your heart to claim . . .

The words struck Bethany with bitter force. Her mild wooing was certainly all in vain. Shaun would never love her nor try to claim her heart. She'd have to keep reminding herself that their relationship was strictly platonic.

But when she looked toward him again from beneath lowered lashes, just the sight of his strong brow topped by that untamed mop of black hair set her pulse to racing in time to the lilting song.

When the medley ended at last, the room erupted in spontaneous applause. Mrs. Rosselli bowed her acknowledgment and launched into a new song that Shaun said was by a composer named Rossini. The beauty of the music lifted Bethany out of her temporary depression. Even though she knew Shaun did not love her, she could still enjoy the music, the elegant surroundings, the promise of delicious food.

When the waiter finally wheeled in a cart bearing four plates covered with silver lids, the subtle but spicy aroma wafting from the plates made Bethany's mouth water at the prospect of the fulfillment of that promise. Mrs. Rosselli took a break from entertaining the customers and left the stage to join her family.

Before beginning the meal, Shaun and his parents joined hands, bowing their heads briefly in prayer. Shaun clasped one of Bethany's hands and Mr. Rosselli the other to include her in the silent blessing. Again, it seemed so natural, so matter-of-fact, for them to honor God in this simple way, that Bethany felt deeply moved. At the same time her old guilt nagged at the back of her mind. Would Shaun be shocked if she revealed she hadn't been inside a church in many months? Would he ever understand the doubts that had plagued her for so long, the sense of separation she felt not only from her mother, whom she hadn't seen in over a year, but from God, as well?

Soon her anxiety vanished in the glory of tender

veal smothered with melted mozzarella cheese and a tangy tomato sauce blended with herbs and spices, garnished with sprigs of bright green parsley, as pretty to look at as it proved delectable. The meal was accompanied by large green salads, crisp and fresh, and individual loaves of warm bread with buttery brown crusts.

At last, replete with food, Bethany sat back in her chair and said, "Mr. Rosselli, I've never before eaten anything this good in my entire life!"

"Told you so!" Shaun gloated.

Not wanting to exclude Mrs. Rosselli from the compliments, Bethany turned to her and continued, "And your voice is simply breath-taking." To Shaun, she concluded, "Yes, you're right, your parents are wonderful."

Shaun shrugged. "Any couple who could produce such an exceptionally handsome son with such a fine head of hair would have to be special—"

"Oh, you!" she interrupted, reaching out to punch him lightly on the arm.

He flinched in mock fear. "Mom, she's hitting me again!"

"And rightly so," his mother stated calmly. "You're totally conceited and deserve to be smacked at least once a day."

They could joke about it, Bethany thought, because, for them, smacking had *not* been an every day occurrence as it had for her when she was young. Seeing Mrs. Rosselli, so regal yet so warm and open, turned Bethany's thoughts to her own mother. What might she be doing at this moment? Did the thin nervous woman she remembered with such mixed feelings ever think about her daughter? Did she feel remorse for all the unhappiness she'd inflicted during one of her "spells?" Well, it wasn't worth thinking about now. Bethany had severed all ties many months before, and had no intention of ever going home again.

And yet hearing Shaun banter with his parents with such affection opened an aching void somewhere deep inside her, making her aware that something was missing in her life. She realized that it was the child inside her still crying out for love and acceptance.

Surreptitiously she lowered her hands to her lap and opened her purse. She felt around until her fingers closed about the bag that held the sand dollar. What was the legend . . . that the five slits around the edge stood for the nail holes in Christ's hands and feet and the wound in his side? Christ had suffered too, at the hands of those who should have loved him, and yet he had been able to forgive. If she could just forgive . . .

No, protested a voice inside her head. *Some things just can't be forgiven! Jesus was God. He had the power to overcome His pain. I'm just a human being, one person in this big cruel world, and I'll never forgive, never!*

Even as she thought the bitter words, another picture formed in her mind—the five white doves nestled inside the delicate shell, carrying God's message of peace and good will to all His people. It was true. In the Bible stories she'd heard in Sunday school when she was a child, God often sent His message in care of a dove. What would God do now, if He were here in her place? He would forgive her mother, she suspected. Yet she couldn't do that. She'd been too deeply hurt by the one person in the world who should have been her protector and her greatest comfort.

She closed her purse again and forced a smile as she listened to Mr. Rosselli tell about his boyhood in Italy. When he began to describe a trip to Florence, where he had viewed paintings and sculptures by Michaelangelo and Leonardo da Vinci, her attention was totally captured at last, and she forgot her own problems in her excitement over the artistic wonders he had seen.

"And all I do is illustrate sympathy cards," she sighed when he had finished.

"I'd like to hear about that," Mrs. Rosselli encouraged.

Feeling a bit shy, Bethany described her Bible and candle design to be printed on gold foil, which the committee had approved during their critique session earlier that week.

"Of course I dream of doing something really significant someday—of creating a painting that will inspire others the way 'The Last Supper' has inspired viewers for centuries," she said, and then paused, embarrassed that they might think she was comparing herself to the great da Vinci.

But Shaun just nodded as he asked, "Have you seen the life-size sculptures in wood of all the figures from 'The Last Supper' on display in one of the churches down near the Country Club Plaza?"

When she said no, he continued, "They're spectacular. I'll take you there sometime. Meanwhile . . . " He surveyed her speculatively. "Well, who knows, your mural at the hospital may change some lives too, in ways you can't yet see."

She appreciated the thought, and wished she would

feel the same degree of confidence. Nevertheless, she experienced a shiver of anticipation at the idea of painting that large white wall.

The rest of the evening went very smoothly. When Shaun walked her to her door, she realized it had been a long time since she'd had so much fun.

"Hope you haven't forgotten I need to come in and pick up the sketches," he reminded her as she turned the key in the lock.

"I hadn't forgotten," she said, flashing him a smile. "Oh, I do hope the board members will like them."

Once inside, she bustled about, gathering up the drawings and slipping them into a portfolio. She was intensely aware of Shaun as he worked beside her, of the rustling of his jacket and the smell of his after shave lotion, musky and male.

"Well, that's it," she said at last, holding out the heavy portfolio with both hands.

He took the portfolio and set it down on a chair. Before she realized what was happening, he had swept her into his arms and was holding her close against the thudding of his heart.

"Bethany," he murmured softly. "There's a mystery about you . . . I don't know what it is, but I felt drawn to you the first moment I saw you. When I thought you were going to jump that day—and that I might not get there in time . . ."

He buried his face in her hair, continuing to hold her in a tight embrace. Within the circle of his arms, Bethany felt protected and warmed by his concern. His breath, more of a long sigh, stirred her hair like the caress of a gentle wind, sending tingles down her neck. She leaned against him, comforted by his strength. For the first time in her life Bethany yearned to know the bliss that could result from the union of a man and woman in harmony with God's age-old plan.

When Shaun released her and stepped away, she quickly clutched the edge of the table, taking a deep breath as she forced strength back into her knees. Did he know the effect his embrace had had upon her, she wondered, unable for a moment to look at him. Finally she glanced up and found him gazing at her with that amazing blue blaze of fire that always surprised her, even now. Eyes such as his were too brilliant to be real; they looked more like an artist's idealized concept of what eyes should be.

"Bethany, . . ." he began, but paused before going on. When he finally continued, she got the impression he had started to say something else, something more personal, but had changed his mind. "I'll call you tomorrow morning as soon as the board makes a decision. If they approve, and I see no reason why they wouldn't, maybe you could come on out tomorrow afternoon and get started."

All she could do was to nod in reply, not yet trusting her voice. But when he picked up the portfolio and moved toward the door, she was able to pull herself together at last. She followed him. "Thank you for a lovely evening, Shaun. I had a wonderful time."

"So did I."

He smiled down at her, a warm intimate smile that seemed to initiate background music for Bethany, as though she had suddenly been transported into the middle of an old-fashioned movie set.

"Well, see you tomorrow," he continued.

He reached out and briefly touched her cheek once more with a caressing fingertip. Then he was gone.

She locked the door and leaned her forehead for a moment against the cool surface of the wood. Emotions whirled about inside like a tornado on a hot summer afternoon. There was no way he could ever really love her, of course. She knew that. She wasn't worthy of love—never had been. He might admire her as an artist, might even be somewhat attracted to her but she could hope for no more.

Why couldn't she accept that; why did she keep hoping . . . ? But there was no point in pursuing the thought.

Suddenly feeling very tired, she prepared for bed, hoping that sleep would bring peace. Instead, it brought a nightmare painted in feverish colors. While she shrank back in terror, flames shot from the fingers of her left hand. She watched with disbelief while her arm melted, shriveling into a black stick. In the background she heard her mother's voice crooning, "No one will ever love you, no one. . . ."

She awoke, drenched in perspiration. The horror of the dream clung about her like a dark cloak.

You're wrong, mother. He will love me. You'll see! she wanted to shout. But she wasn't sure. It was a long hour before she slept again.

CHAPTER 5

WHEN THE PHONE RANG during the noon hour the next day, Bethany lifted the receiver to hear Shaun's excited voice. "You're in!"

"Wha . . . "

"The board—they accepted you! So how about it? Can you start this afternoon?"

A thrill shot along Bethany's nerves. "You mean it?"

"The sooner Bobby can get going on this project, the better. If you can come, I'll wait here at the hospital and stay with you through this first session."

Elation at the prospect of seeing Shaun again soared through Bethany like a bird's sudden flight. "I'll grab a bite to eat and be right there."

"That's my girl!"

My girl—if only that could be true. But she knew his words were just a casual expression, devoid of meaning.

She quickly made and ate a sandwich, then put

together a box of supplies: felt tip pens, water colors and brushes, pencils with thick soft leads, a sketch book, sheets of newsprint, a plastic pitcher and several plastic cups, a roll of masking tape, and a couple of old shirts to use for painting smocks. She packed her car and then drove through the busy streets with the lilting melody of *The Habanera* running through her mind: "Love's a bird so free and wild, a bird that one can never tame . . . "

She remembered her defiant thoughts from the night before: *He will love me, you'll see.*

Could she possibly tame the bird of love? She suspected that her lack of experience prevented her from reading Shaun's responses correctly. What did he *really* feel for her? She wished she knew. . . . When she pulled into the parking lot and saw him waiting there to meet her, her nerves flashed as though she had touched a bare electrical wire. She found she was actually shaking when she climbed from the car to greet him.

But his smile was open, without any sign of flirtation as he announced, "Decided to come out and watch for you. Here, I'll help you carry your things."

She opened the trunk and handed him the box of art supplies. Her fingers accidentally brushed his when he took the box from her and she caught her breath in a slight gasp. As she locked her car, she was grateful that he hadn't seemed to notice her reaction.

"I've told Bobby you're coming," Shaun said. "He's really excited about it, and so am I. Bethany, I feel that this project will lead to a major breakthrough for him. What a miracle if that can happen! I sometimes think that running into you on top of City Hall that day was meant to be—that the good Lord had this plan in mind all along."

76

He led Bethany into the building where Bobby was housed, to a large room with two long tables arranged in a "T" shape, with chairs set up as though for a conference.

"This is where we hold our board meetings," he explained. "I thought this would be a good place for you and Bobby to work. I'll ring for a nurse to bring him down."

Shaun stepped to an intercom box attached to one wall and punched several buttons. Speaking briefly with the person who answered, he turned back to Bethany and remarked with a smile of anticipation, "The nurse says Bobby can hardly wait. He knows he's going to get to draw while he's with you. Drawing seems to be what he lives for."

Soon the motherly nurse whom Bethany had met the preceding weekend entered, holding Bobby's hand. Large fearful eyes peered out of a pinched, pale face. Bobby seemed even more vulnerable than Bethany had remembered. She wanted to put her arms around him and hold him, but knew that taking such a liberty prematurely might frighten him and do more harm than good.

She pointed to the box that was now sitting on one of the tables. "Bobby, I've brought you a surprise. Do you want to look in there and see what it is?"

For one second he resisted, searching Bethany's face with eyes filled with distrust. Then, at Shaun's gentle urging, he approached the table cautiously and climbed up into a chair to peer into the box.

"Oh!"

The exclamation exploded from him like air rushing out of a balloon. He reached into the box and took out a fat black felt-tipped pen. He pulled off the cap with his teeth and immediately drew a slash across the cast on his arm.

"Not on the cast, Bobby. See? Here's some paper I've brought just for you."

Bethany taped a large sheet of newsprint to the table in front of the boy. He began drawing at once—another horse similar to the one he'd drawn on the restroom wall. The horse's head lifted toward the sky while its mane and tail blew wildly in the wind, portrayed by a few sweeping marks across the page. Bethany felt a thrill of pleasure as she watched the boy work.

When he finished that picture, she quickly took up the sheet and taped a second in its place, then arranged the rest of the felt-tipped pens in a rainbow-colored fan near Bobby's left arm, ready for his use. He removed all the caps and set to work on a new picture, a landscape filled with animals in various colors: a pink cat, an orange squirrel, a yellow bird, a green mouse, each one with its own special character, so alive that Bethany and Shaun both broke into delighted laughter.

"Okay, Bobby, now I want to draw a picture for you," Bethany said as she taped down a clean sheet. She quickly drew several vertical lines in the middle of the page. "What does that look like?"

Bobby studied them seriously. "A road?"

"Could be. Anything else?"

"A fence?"

Bethany smiled, pleased that he had given her the opening she'd hoped for.

"Yes, that could be a fence. Let me tell you a story about a boy and a fence."

She began sketching in quick free strokes as she recited the tale of Tom Sawyer and the white-washed fence, keeping the story simple so Bobby's attention wouldn't wander. As the boys in their overalls and battered hats took shape in the picture, Bobby began to grin.

"But I really think this picture needs a dog, don't you?" Bethany said as she handed him the pen. "Right there, at the end of the fence . . . will you draw it for me?"

He took the pen without hesitation and sketched in the dog, its tongue lolling out of its mouth as it frisked on two hind legs, tail curled upward in a cheerful arc.

"Good boy!" Bethany exclaimed, clasping her hands together and shaking them in a victory sign.

But Bobby's face clouded. "No, Bad Boy," he said as he pointed at the dog.

Oh, no! Bethany thought with dismay. She realized that they were right back where they'd started when he'd drawn that dog the week before. Shaun stepped in at once, taking a clean sheet of paper and changing the subject adroitly. "Hey, Bobby, can you draw a truck?"

Diverted, the boy took another pen and began covering the page with trucks, cars and planes. Bethany got her own sketch book and started a series of quick sketches of Bobby himself—from the side, the front, the back—capturing his boyish posture as he bent, absorbed, over his pictures. After doing several studies of his profile, she added, on one, a straw hat and a bandana scarf in the style of Huckleberry Finn.

Shaun drew near to watch her work. She smelled again the scent of his lotion, but she didn't allow that to distract her as she concentrated on her sketches. She felt pleased, sure of herself now as she exercised the skills she had gained through four years of college training, followed by her apprenticeship with the advertising agency and now her months with the King Card Company. When Bobby finally filled his page and sat back to survey his work, she held out her own pad at arms' length to examine with narrowed eyes the total effect of her drawings.

"Excellent!" Shaun exclaimed, his voice warm with admiration. "Bethany, you amaze me with your talent. How do you know exactly where to place the lines, how to translate what you see to the surface of the paper?"

Bethany smiled, pleased by his praise. "It's hard to explain. I just look and somehow my hand begins to move. It's as though my fingers are attached directly to my eyes, I feel a stirring in my hand, and the pencil glides over the paper, and I *feel* what's happening there. Sometimes I don't even have to look down, I'm so sure."

She paused, suddenly shy about the uncharacteristic torrent of words. Would he think her egotistical? She didn't mean it that way—

But he returned the smile warmly. "God has given you a special gift," he said softly. "You've been blessed, Bethany, in a unique and wonderful way."

Again, she was confounded by his faith, so much a part of his life that he spoke without embarrassment or hesitation. She had felt, sometimes, as though her inspiration came from somewhere outside herself, as though she were being guided by an unseen power. Could that power possibly be God? Could she allow herself to take that "leap of faith" that she'd sometimes heard ministers talk about, and accept that a loving God had given her artistic talent for a special reason—that perhaps—just perhaps He considered Bethany herself special?

"And, Bobby, you have a God-given talent, too," Shaun continued gently. "You'll make a fine artist one day."

Bobby slid his eyes sideways and peered up at Shaun like a wary little animal waiting to see if that big creature nearby was going to pounce. After a moment, the wariness left his eyes and a grin spread across his face.

Bethany handed Shaun the plastic pitcher. "Could you get us some water and some paper towels?"

"Sure, be right back."

By the time Shaun returned, Bethany had taped several more sheets of paper to the table.

"We'll work with poster paints now," she told the child. "They're lots of fun."

She draped one of the old shirts around Bobby's neck to protect his clothes, then handed him a large brush. Mixing powdered pigments in the various cups she'd brought, she added clear water and stirred. Soon Bobby was splashing paint across the sheets, laughing with glee when the colors ran together and spread out in abstract shapes. He had a natural sense of design, adding splotches of color here and there to balance out the patterns. Shaun untaped one especially bright composition and laid it to one side.

"I'm going to mat and frame that one for my office," he said. "It's as good as some I've seen for sale at the Art Fair in the Country Club Plaza."

The afternoon went by faster than Bethany could have imagined. While Bobby worked enthusiastically with the materials, Bethany continued her own sketches, capturing the child in various poses. It was Shaun who finally called a halt, explaining that Bobby needed to clean up and get ready for dinner. The three of them worked together to straighten the room, then

Shaun called the nurse to come for Bobby. She exclaimed with delight over his paintings and took a couple back with her to tape to the wall of the playroom.

"Goodbye, Bobby," Bethany said as he started to leave. She risked planting a quick kiss on the top of his head that he accepted without flinching.

One small step forward, she thought in triumph.

As Shaun helped carry her supplies out to the car, she watched him from the corner of her eye, trying not to be obvious. The way he moved, at ease with himself and yet revealing a hint of pent-up power, sent her pulse racing in her veins like a swollen brook after a warm July rain.

"Dr. Rosselli!"

Shaun's name, shrilled in an angry voice, startled Bethany. She whirled to see a woman, thin and unkempt, step from around a car to come striding in their direction. The woman's stringy red hair had slipped from a careless attempt at a ponytail to hang untidily about her pale freckled face. She wore ragged cut-off jeans and a man's shirt, stained down the front and missing a button. The gray rubber thongs that protected her dusty feet slapped against the asphalt. Even before Shaun spoke, Bethany knew she had to be Bobby's mother. The resemblance was too strong.

"Mrs. Ryan . . . ," Shaun began, but the woman interrupted harshly.

"When are you lettin' Bobby outta there?"

"You know we can't—"

"Can't what? Can't trust him with me? Is that what you were gonna say?" The woman's face flushed a dark red. "I'm sick and tired of you people interferin' with me and my kid. He's a bad boy and has to be made to mind, that's all."

Bethany's stomach twisted into a knot and a sourness stung her throat. "So you break his arm, is that it?" Her voice rasped through the air like a knife. "You think the way to discipline a child is to hurt him like that?"

The woman turned blazing eyes upon Bethany. "Who are *you* ?"

Shaun stepped aside to lay the box on the hood of the car, then turned back to Bethany and took her arm in a quieting gesture. "Mrs. Ryan, we . . . ."

"This ain't none of her business," the woman insisted angrily. "What right does she have, speakin' up like that?"

Bethany knew she should keep still, and yet her sense of outrage overcame her discretion. "I'm a friend of Bobby's, that's who I am," she said firmly. "I can't stand to see a child mistreated—"

"All I done was try to get him to behave. That's my job," the woman replied, fixing Bethany with a narrow-eyed look. "People all the time sayin' I ain't a fit mother. Well, let me tell you, it ain't easy raisin' a kid alone!"

Shaun gently moved Bethany to one side, then stepped forward to face the glowering woman.

"Look, Mrs. Ryan, we know you've had a hard time, but what we're trying to do here is help both you and Bobby. You missed your last counseling session. If you want Bobby back, you're going to have to come for therapy—you know that."

How can he keep so calm! Bethany thought as she fought against the anger seething inside. What she wanted to do was tell Mrs. Ryan off, make the woman admit what a terrible person she was.

"Your next appointment is . . . next Tuesday afternoon, right?" Shaun asked. When the woman nodded sullenly, he continued, "Come in then and we'll talk about this some more. You've been hurt pretty badly yourself in the past. That's why you have these problems now. . . ."

To Bethany's surprise, the woman's eyes filled with tears.

"Nobody knows what I been through," she said in a whining voice. "People's done me wrong—"

Shaun let go of Bethany's arm and stepped forward to lay a comforting hand on Mrs. Ryan's shoulder.

"I'm sure some people have hurt you. And if you let us talk with you about it, we'll try to help you get your life turned around. Next Tuesday, okay?" He patted her shoulder and repeated in a firmer tone, "Will we see you then, Mrs. Ryan?"

"Well . . . " The woman fidgeted, pulling her brows together in a frown. "Well, I guess so."

"Good. See you on Tuesday." Shaun picked up the box and added, "Come on, Bethany, let's get these things loaded."

After casting one more unfriendly look in Bethany's direction, the woman turned and slouched off, her thongs slapping against the surface of the parking lot. She climbed into an old blue Volkswagen with a dented red fender and ground the gears before rattling off.

"What a disgusting woman!" Bethany exploded. "How can you even *think* of giving Bobby back to her?"

"The courts make that decision," Shaun reminded her quietly. "Whenever possible, they try to get families back together. Mrs. Ryan loves Bobby—"

"*Loves him?*" Bethany snorted with disbelief. "Do you really expect me to believe that?!"

"Yes, she does. And Bobby loves her—"

"He can't possibly."

"He's scared, and he's confused. But he does love her. What we have to do is try to change their behavior . . ."

"It would take a miracle to do that!"

"It just might," Shaun replied seriously. "Please pray about it, Bethany. We need all the help we can get."

"You really think prayer will help?" Bethany could no longer keep the skepticism from her voice.

"Of course. Sometimes it's the only thing that will." Shaun turned to give Bethany a penetrating look. "I sense a hurt in you that goes much deeper than your grief for Bobby, and I think it has something to do with your own past. Want to talk about it?"

Bethany flared indignantly at his probing. "You're imagining things!"

"No, I don't think so."

They'd reached her car by then. Shaun deposited the box on the trunk and turned to take hold of her left wrist, pointing to the burn scars there.

"Did your mother do this to you?"

Quickly she snatched her hand away. "I'm not your patient!" she protested, feeling the hot tears spring to her eyes. Annoyed with herself, she dashed the tears away. "Save your questions for someone else, would you please, doctor? I don't need your help."

She picked up the box and balanced it on one hip while unlocking the trunk, then placed the box inside and slammed the lid. Emotions churned within in heated waves, making her heart race and her skin burn. A part of her wanted to fall against his shoulder and have his strong arms surround her in loving comfort. Another part of her argued resentfully, *It's none of his business. Who does he think he is?*

She had a feeling of *déjà vu* and realized that she was reacting in the same defensive way as had Mrs. Ryan just minutes before.

"When you're hurting, it hurts me, too. Don't you know that by now?" he asked softly.

She leaned against the trunk, still not looking at him. She felt his hands on her shoulders, and again she yearned to have him hold her against the strong thud of his heart; but a sudden vivid picture of him touching Mrs. Ryan's shoulder made Bethany wonder if he were patronizing her too. She slipped away from him to climb into her car.

"Bethany, don't go yet . . . ."

But she turned the key in the ignition, ignoring his plea, desperate to escape his questioning, and the probing blue eyes that seemed able to penetrate the secret recesses of her mind. She hadn't driven more than three blocks, however before reason returned.

You thought you could tame the bird of love? she asked herself in derision. *Well, you just shot it down. He offered to help, and you rejected him. How could you be so stupid?*

She pounded one fist against the steering wheel in frustration, knowing she did not want to tell him anything about her past, but wishing she'd handled it differently.

Maybe he'll call. . . .

And if he did, what would she say? How could she ever apologize for her rudeness?

By the time she reached home, she'd played the scene over and over in her mind, thinking of other responses she could have made, statements that would at least have allowed him to keep some respect for her. As it was, he probably now saw her as as an overgrown but immature child.

The phone started ringing just after she entered her apartment. Her heart leapt erratically at the sound, hoping that it might be Shaun yet fearing the hope would be realized.

"Oh, good, you're home! I've tried to call you three times. Bethany, I'm sorry—"

His familiar voice, filled with concern, poured into her ear when she lifted the receiver.

"I'm the one who was rude. I'm the one who's sorry!" she exclaimed, surprised by his apology. "Shaun, I know you only wanted to help—"

"But I pushed you when you're not yet ready to talk," he replied. "I just wanted to be sure you're okay . . ."

"Yes, I'm fine," she said. "No problem." *Which is an out-and-out lie,* chided her inner voice.

Shaun's words seemed to her to carry an undercurrent of patronizing, which she deeply resented. . . . *Not yet ready to talk,* he'd said, as though he felt sure that one day she *would* be ready to talk to him. The great doctor was always at work, looking beneath the surface, analyzing, dissecting her emotions as though she were some kind of laboratory insect. If their meeting on top of City Hall had indeed been a part of God's plan, as Shaun seemed to believe, then what was the purpose behind it all? What possible good could come of dredging into the mud of the past?

"I didn't mean to sound so ungrateful a while ago in the parking lot," she went on, keeping her tone light. "I know you just wanted to help me, but there's no need for you to worry. I burned my wrist in an accident long ago, that's all. No big deal."

"That's okay. I understand," he said.

His tone implied that he suspected there was more to the story than she was revealing. Ignoring that, she made one or two casual comments about the progress on the mural, then bid Shaun goodnight. After hanging up, she leaned her forehead against the heels of her hands and closed her eyes. Anxiety nibbled at the back of her mind like a mouse worrying a morsel of cheese. If she didn't break things off with Shaun right then, she knew she was in danger of succumbing to his gentle but insistent questioning.

I should call him back and say that I've changed my mind, that I can no longer work on the project, she told herself.

But never to see Shaun again, his gem-fire eyes, his flyaway hair, never to hear his warm deep voice, which could be tender at times, teasing at others? The thought chilled her, as though she'd just been told the sun had gone away, leaving the earth in darkness.

No, she couldn't tell him goodbye, not yet, for she was drawn to him as to no other man she'd ever met. But she *could* set a guard on her feelings, starting right away.

Holding tight to that resolve, she went to bed.

CHAPTER 6

THE IDEA FOR THE PICNIC came to Bethany about three weeks later. By then, she'd started working evenings as well as weekends at the hospital, sketching the outline for the mural in charcoal on the dining room wall, preparatory to letting Bobby help her fill in the large areas with paint. She kept the boy near her whenever she worked, showing him how a mural is planned and letting him practice filling in shapes with paint on large sheets of brown paper. He proved to be an apt student, absorbing information the way Bethany's cleanup sponges absorbed water. As his confidence and trust increased, he finally began to talk with Bethany who had, for a while, despaired of ever breaking through the boy's protective shell.

"Hey, Bethany, tell me that part again . . . you know, where Huck and Tom build that raft and float down the river," Bobby asked one Saturday afternoon, his brown eyes gleaming with anticipation as he peered at Bethany from beneath the old-fashioned

"Huckleberry Finn" straw hat that Shaun had given him.

Bethany grinned at him fondly. "You like that part, don't you? Okay, one more time . . ."

Laying aside her long stick of soft gray charcoal, she sat down beside the child and launched once more into the adventures of the two boys immortalized so long ago by Mark Twain.

When she finished recreating that vivid scene, Bobby sighed, "I'd like to go on a raft sometime."

That's when the idea came to Bethany. "We can't ride on a raft, but we *can* go on a picnic," she said enthusiastically. "I know a place on top of a cliff overlooking the river where you could watch the boats go by. It's a perfect picnic spot."

Then she remembered that Bobby was confined to the hospital and that there might be red tape involved in his release for a day's outing.

"We'll have to check with Dr. Rosselli first, though, to see if it's okay. But if I can get permission, would you like to go?"

"You bet I would. I ain't never been on a picnic!"

Later, when Bethany brought up the idea to Shaun, he was enthusiastic. "I'll have to ask the hospital director about it," he said, "but I see no reason why a picnic can't be arranged. I'd better go along, though, just in case any problems come up. Bobby's doing a whole lot better, thanks to you, but he still has his moments."

Bethany felt a flare of excitement at the news that Shaun would be coming along. To picnic with him atop a wind-swept river bluff beneath blue skies and towering cumulous clouds . . . the prospect kept her awake for over an hour in bed that night.

The next afternoon as she hurried down the corridor toward the dining room at the hospital, she bumped unexpectedly into Shaun who beamed with pleasure when he told her that the director had approved the picnic.

"Everyone who works with Bobby has noticed the change in him since you came," Shaun told her warmly. "He's cooperating now, draws on the paper instead of the floors, and he talks all the time—about you, and about Tom Sawyer . . . the nurses say they can't get him to shut up! Very unlike the old Bobby who rarely said a word. Now he seems to be trying to make up for lost time. I don't think his mother ever talked to him much, except to yell—"

"That woman!" Bethany interrupted fiercely. "Shaun, *why* does he have to go back to her?"

"I've told you already—"

"I know what you told me, but I still don't like it. Is there any chance for a real change?"

"Well, we're working on it."

"Are you making any progress?"

"Some. His mother has had a hard time of it, Bethany. She was an abused child herself—had a father who beat her all the time. And then she married a man who turned out to be an abuser, too. Often happens that way, I'm sad to say. But she *does* want to change. We're helping her to recognize the signals in herself that lead to an explosion, and we're giving her tools for learning to turn that behavior around. And there's a church group working with her now—a Bible study class. The women in that group are giving her a lot of support."

If there had been someone like that for *her* own mother, maybe her childhood would have been much different, Bethany thought wistfully. For the first time she wondered about the motivation behind her mother's actions. Could there have been something in her mother's background that caused her to lose control when the going got rough? Well, it was too late to find out now. After a year of no communication, Bethany suspected that her mother had written her out of her life. Better to leave well enough alone.

And this conversation had gone far enough, too, Bethany told herself. Time to change the subject before Shaun started quizzing her again.

"So when can we go—next Saturday?" she asked. "I hope the day is nice. Have you heard a long-term weather forecast on TV?"

Shaun grinned. "Wouldn't do any good if I had. You know what they say about Missouri weather— wait five minutes and it will change. But, yes, I think next Saturday would be just fine. What do you want me to bring?"

"Just yourself. I'll fix the food—I have a new sandwich spread recipe I've been wanting to try out."

"You know, this really sounds like fun! I haven't been on a picnic in a long time." The blue of his eyes darkened with visible emotion as he stared down at Bethany. "Bobby's not the only one who's changed since meeting you, did you know that? I look at the world with new eyes now—I see colors I've never noticed before, I see the landscape arranged in patterns like a painting . . . and I've been reading all of Mark Twain's books again. I'd forgotten what a good writer he was. Makes me want to take off from work and go drifting in a boat down that lazy old Missouri River. But a picnic by the river will be fun, too. Thanks for thinking of it, Bethany. And thanks for letting me come along.''

As though I would have kept you away! Bethany yearned for one brief moment to have Shaun all to herself on the river bluffs. To stretch out on a blanket beside him while watching the cloud formations change shape overhead—

The intimate picture filled her with a rush of warmth. Shaun began to grin as though he could read her thoughts. ''Maybe sometime we can have another picnic and leave Bobby behind,'' he said, surprising her with the accuracy of his perception.

He bent and kissed her on the cheek. The contact startled her, leaving her breathless.

''Do you know how beautiful you are?'' he murmured softly.

Filled with confusion, she couldn't answer.

''Yes, Bethany—*you*—beautiful inside and out,'' he continued, gazing down at her fervently. ''You have a beautiful spirit. I could see that right from the start. The way you volunteered to help Bobby as soon as I asked you—that was a real blessing.''

She felt like a hypocrite as she stood, still silent, listening to his praise. For she remembered that it wasn't her altruistic spirit that had prompted her to accept the challenge of working with Bobby, but the hypnotic attraction of Shaun's heaven-blue eyes.

''I'm the one who's blessed,'' she replied at last. ''I think I'm learning more from Bobby than he is from me.''

Shaun nodded his agreement. ''I know what you mean. I learn something new every day. Which reminds me—'' he glanced at his watch and then made a wry face—''I'm already late for a counseling session with a parent who can only come in after his working hours.'' He shook his head as he gazed down at her. ''You're a distracting element, Bethany!''

He brushed her cheek with his fingertips and then hurried away, leaving her skin tingling deliciously from his touch. When she set to work on the cartoon for the mural, she sketched a bird that was too big for the space and had to rub it out and start over.

Chagrined, she shook her head, murmuring, ''You distract me, too, Shaun Churchill Rosselli!''

CHAPTER 7

THE DAY OF THE PICNIC dawned with golden promise—not a cloud in the sky.

After breakfast, Bethany whistled happily as she prepared the sandwiches from ham and chicken spreads she'd made the night before, using recipes she'd clipped from a magazine to save for a special occasion. She layered chopped tomatoes and alfalfa sprouts over the mixtures for garnish, instead of lettuce, and carefully sliced the sandwiches into manageable halves. Just in case, she included several peanut butter and jelly sandwiches for Bobby, then placed all the wrapped sandwiches on top of a sack of ice in the large insulation-lined wicker picnic basket, along with a fried chicken, three large red apples, and a carton of butter pecan ice cream as a special surprise for Shaun. In a separate sack she placed a thermos of iced tea and another of chocolate milk, a bag of home-baked chocolate chip cookies, a red-checked tablecloth with matching napkins, red plastic cups, and white plastic forks and spoons.

That should hold two hungry men! she thought with satisfaction as she surveyed her handiwork.

When the doorbell rang she straightened her jeans over her slim hips and tucked one errant corner of her red bandana cloth blouse back under her tooled leather belt before hurrying to open the door. Shaun and Bobby stood there hand-in-hand with big smiles on their faces.

"See?" Bobby proudly lifted his right arm and wiggled his fingers to show Bethany that his cast had been removed.

"Oh, honey, that's wonderful! Now we *really* have cause to celebrate! Come on in, you two. Everything's ready."

They followed her into the kitchen where Shaun lifted the "ice chest" basket from the table, grunting with surprise at its weight.

"How many people were you planning to feed today—the whole U.S. army?"

"Nope, just one big man and one hungry boy," Bethany replied cheerfully.

"And one good-looking female," Shaun added, eyeing her trim figure with appreciation. "Looks as if an extra pound or two wouldn't hurt a thing!"

She welcomed Bobby's interruption at that moment, "What can I carry?" he demanded, holding out his hands.

"Can you manage a sack with two thermos bottles in it?"

"I sure can. I'm just as good as new."

"Okay, then," she said, placing the sack carefully in his arms.

When the car was loaded, they headed east on the highway out of the city. The bluff Bethany had in mind was one where she'd picnicked before—a beautiful spot with a good view of the river and the rolling plains beyond.

On the way, filled with exuberant spirits, they sang "Old McDonald Had A Farm," running through all the ordinary farm animals—cow, horse, sheep, goat, pig, chicken, duck—before Shaun started adding animals that Farmer McDonald had probably never thought of. He imported an elephant, a camel, a tiger and a lion, roaring or trumpeting with such enthusiasm that Bethany and Bobby broke up in laughter.

As they left the highway to drive through the rich Missouri farmland, Bobby suddenly pointed toward a shaggy beast standing near a fence.

"What's that?"

"Looks as though this 'Old McDonald' has a buffalo," Shaun replied with a grin while reaching out to ruffle Bobby's red hair.

Bethany watched the two of them from the corner of her eye. She found herself fantasizing that Shaun was her husband and Bobby, her son. Suddenly she felt an overwhelming surge of love for both of them, a yearning that in its intensity was almost physical pain. She saw a three-bedroom ranch-style house near enough to the city for Shaun to commute to the hospital, yet far enough out in the country for Bobby to keep several pets, maybe even a buffalo. She would build a painting studio on the north side of the house, for even year-round light, with floor-to-ceiling windows. . . .

A touch on her shoulder brought her back with a start from her dream world.

"Junction ahead. Do we go left or right?" Shaun asked.

"Left. After about a quarter of a mile, head north again down a dirt road. Takes us to the meadow above the bluff."

"How did you find out about this place, anyway?"

Bethany smiled, remembering. "I could try to be mysterious and spin you a tale. But the truth is, all this land belongs to the boss of that advertising firm I used to work for—back before I got my job at King. He brought all his employees here one weekend for a big barbecue and I fell in love with the view. He said I could picnic here anytime."

"Your old boss, eh?" Shaun flashed her a quizzical look. "Is he young? Good-looking? Rich? Does he have lots of hair?"

Bethany laughed at Shaun's "third degree." He was only pretending to be jealous, she could see, and yet she detected a touch of true anxiety beneath his facetious tone.

"Middle-aged. Short and fat. Probably in debt. Bald," she said, answering his questions in order.

"Now that last answer worries me." He frowned, but she spotted a twinkle in his eyes. "It's those bald ones you have to watch out for—they're real lover boys."

"Is that a personal prophecy—that when you're bald, you'll be a lover boy?" she teased back.

"I hope so—if I'm with the right girl."

Again, she felt breathless and nonplussed. Did he mean that she was the right girl, or was she reading between the lines? *He will love me, you'll see*—her own words rang once more in her mind. Now he seemed to be echoing them yet she couldn't accept it,

98

couldn't bring herself to believe that she deserved to be happy. She bent to adjust Bobby's seat belt, using the task as an excuse to break contact with Shaun's challenging smile.

"Are we almost there?" Bobby bounced eagerly against the restraining grip of the belt.

"Just about."

"Will we see Huck and Tom on their raft?"

"No, but we'll watch other boats go by while we eat our lunch."

"Did you put in chocolate chip cookies?"

"Sure did! Baked 'em last night."

"I'm hungry already!"

"Me, too," Shaun chimed in.

Bethany shook her head in mock exasperation. "It's a good thing I *did* pack enough for the U.S. Army. Okay, there's the lane just ahead."

Shaun turned onto the grassy track, no more than two shallow ruts overgrown with weeds that soon ended at the edge of the broad wind-swept meadow Bethany remembered so well from the barbecue. The meadow sloped gently down the hilltop to the edge of the bluff where a gnarled cedar, ragged with age, reached into space above the river. Shaun parked the car and they climbed out beneath the translucent blue glass bowl of the sky that was now laced with wispy strands of white. Bobby lifted both arms in the air, stretching to the limit of his thin body, and then darted off with a whoop to turn several cartwheels in a row.

"Don't go too near the edge of the bluff," Bethany called after him.

His blithe "okay" floated toward her on the wind. Soon he came bounding back as though he had springs on the soles of his sneakers.

"This place is cool! Come on! Let's watch for boats!"

As the three of them descended through the meadow, the view unfolded before them—low rolling hills bordering the other side of the wide expanse of the Missouri River that pushed eastward in a pulsing current, carrying waters that had traveled all the way from Montana, waters that would flow into the Mississippi at St. Louis and eventually find their way to the Louisiana delta, emptying at last into the Gulf of Mexico. The majestic river with its history of adventure, had always fascinated Bethany, and she felt that mystique again as she watched the restless current, once a roadway to steamboats with names like the *Yellowstone*, the *River Queen* and the *Cabanne*.

"Lewis and Clark sailed past here on their way to find the Northwest Passage," she said aloud. "How excited they must have felt, setting off on such a grand adventure."

"Don't forget Huckleberry Finn!" Bobby put in. "Did he go with them, too?"

"No, honey, Huck Finn didn't really live. He's just a character in a story book."

But Bobby's eyes were shining, and Bethany could tell that he had imbued Mark Twain's characters with personalities as real as any of his friends at the hospital.

They came to the edge of the bluff and Bethany was relieved to see that it wasn't as precipitous as she'd remembered. Instead, it fell away in a slope, with shelves of rock, clumps of grass and scraggly shrubs, while below a pile of scree formed a rocky beach beside the swirling waters. A crumbling jetty to one side held a weather-beaten rowboat.

An echoing blast from a horn drew their attention toward the west. A barge laden with coal came poking around the bend. It slid along, riding low as it sought the center of the river, looking like a black, hump-backed sea serpent. A rough brown wake roiled behind, topped with tan colored foam instead of whitecaps. A large man in dusty coveralls waved at them as the barge rolled by, then reached up and tugged on a chain, an action that produced another blast from the horn. Bobby waved his arms so enthusiastically in return that his shoulders seemed to swivel in their sockets.

"I wanna ride on a boat like that," he cried. "I wanna make the horn blow!"

Shaun grinned down at him. "Maybe someday, sport. But now, how about giving that arm some more exercise with a little game of Frisbee?"

They all walked back to the car together and retrieved the food and a large yellow Frisbee that Shaun had brought. While Bethany spread out the lunch on the tablecloth in a flat area near the edge of the bluff, the other two moved back into the meadow where there would be less chance of losing the Frisbee to the river. They sailed the disk back and forth between them, laughing heartily when one or the other failed to catch it.

Trying not to be obvious, Bethany watched Shaun's lithe movements from the corner of her eye, admiring the way his muscles flowed beneath the tight fitting blue knit shirt, revealing the power in his chest and shoulders. When he sprang high in the air, arm reaching for the Frisbee, black curls blowing in tangled protrusion about his forehead, Bethany felt her heart constrict. He caught the disk and sailed it back toward Bobby who loped to catch it, his thin arms and legs flailing in the sun. A picture came to Bethany's mind of a stallion and a colt playing together—the stallion, sure of his power; the colt, still young and awkward. A tenderness toward them both flowed through her like a warm wind.

"Lunch is ready," she called, and they broke off the game to come running with eager smiles.

Bobby plopped himself down on the edge of the cloth and started to reach for a drumstick but Shaun stopped him, taking the boy's hand and then reaching out to Bethany as well. He lifted his face, searching the sky with open eyes as he prayed in a reverent voice, "Oh, Lord, we thank You for this beautiful day. Bless this food of which we are about to partake, and bless the hands that prepared it. We thank You, Lord, for good friends, and ask You to be with us through the rest of this day, and all the days to come. We pray this in Jesus' name. Amen."

"Amen," Bethany echoed, moved by the fervor that had warmed Shaun's voice. She saw that the exertion of the game had shaken the chain from inside his open collar and that the silver cross now gleamed brightly against his chest.

Bobby looked up as Shaun had done, studying the sky with a puzzled frown. "I don't see God nowhere up there."

"You can't *see* God," Shaun told him calmly, "but He's with you just the same. You can talk to Him anytime you want to, no matter where you are."

"I ain't never talked to God," Bobby replied, still frowning. "I can't talk to nobody I can't see."

"Sure you can. Just say, 'Hi, God!' "

"He won't hear me."

"Yes, He will. Trust me."

Skeptically Bobby looked all around. "Hi, God," he said at last.

"There you go," Shaun said cheerfully. "That's all it takes. Whenever you have a problem, just say, 'Hi, God, I need to talk to You.' Then tell Him everything that's bothering you. He does listen, Bobby, he really does."

Bethany watched the gentle expression on Shaun's face as he talked with the boy and felt her heart once more contract with love for them both. Again she allowed herself to envision a home with the three of them in it, living as a family. But Shaun just a few days before had repeated that Bobby would eventually have to return to his mother.

"Hey, let's eat!" Shaun said now, breaking the serious mood as he picked up a piece of chicken and took a bite, then nodded in appreciation. "This is good."

While they ate, they chatted casually with Bobby about his friends at the hospital and Bethany was pleased to see that the boy was eating heartily. At the end, when both the others seemed ready to slow down, she removed the pint sized carton of butter pecan ice cream from its surrounding shell of ice and pulled it out of the basket, "Surprise!"

When she held up the carton, Shaun's eyes widened with pleasure. "You remembered!"

"How could I forget? It's one of the first things I ever learned about you—that you're hung up on butter pecan ice cream."

"That's not the only thing I'm hung up on," he murmured, reaching out to give her hand a squeeze.

She found herself falling once more into the blue depths of his eyes. She wished she could trust her feelings and give herself up to the joy that enveloped her at that moment. But her old doubts about her worthiness hovered behind her like uninvited guests at a feast, cold dark shadows that absorbed the warmth of the sun. She willed the shadows away, forcing herself to smile as Shaun spooned out three portions of the ice cream. Replete at last, they packed the leftovers in the insulated basket, then lay back on the grass and stared contentedly up at the sky. But Bobby couldn't keep still for very long. Soon he was up again, racing about and shouting for them to join him.

"Tag, you're it!" Shaun exclaimed as he jumped to his feet and tapped Bethany on the shoulder.

He darted off across the meadow, heading for a shallow gully. Bethany leapt up and ran after him, with Bobby chasing along behind. Shaun slowed down, perhaps deliberately. Bethany wasn't sure about that. But suddenly he turned, spreading his arms wide, and she ran full tilt into his embrace. The impact threw them both off balance and they fell and tumbled down the grassy slope to land in a tangled heap.

While Bethany scrambled to her knees, she heard Shaun ask anxiously, "Hey, are you all right?"

She brushed her hair back from her eyes and hastened to reassure him. "I'm fine, but what about you?"

"I'm okay."

She saw his face twist with mirth even as his own

laughter bubbled up and spilled over in a merry cascade. He reached out and grabbed her hands, and they laughed together while rocking back and forth on their knees. Then Shaun's laughter faded away and Bethany watched his eyes go smoky and dark with an emotion she'd never seen there before. Her breath caught in her throat when Shaun leaned forward and touched his lips to hers, a kiss so warm and tender that it turned her muscles into mist.

Just then a small body tumbled down to sprawl beside them while a voice piped, "Hey, what are you guys doing?"

The shock of hearing Bobby's voice so close by worked like a douse of icy spray. Bethany quickly pulled away from Shaun, trying to act as though nothing had happened; but she needn't have worried, for Bobby didn't seem too interested in such silly grownup activities.

"Can we go down to the river?" he asked. "I wanna throw rocks in the river."

Shaun rose to his feet and extended a hand to help Bethany up. Self-consciously she smoothed her clothes and hair before meeting Shaun's eyes. He lifted an eyebrow in wry recognition of their narrow escape, then the corners of his mouth quirked up. But Bethany felt her face flame, certain now that he knew her heart, while his gentle kiss had been the impetuous act of any man given the opportunity on an idyllic summer day.

"Throwing rocks in the water—I've always liked to do that, too," Shaun told Bobby in a near normal tone of voice. "How about you, B.C.? You want to join us in a rock-throwing contest?"

It was the first time he'd ever used her old

nickname, and it was certainly the first time she'd ever heard the sound pronounced in such a way that it sounded like a caress. With difficulty she kept her own voice casual. "Sure, that sounds like fun."

They could see now that the gully angled and steepened, cutting a sloping path through the edge of the meadow and down the side of the bluff to the rocky beach below. Scrambling and sliding, they made their way over the water-rounded pebbles and matted piles of leaves and weeds to the fan shaped spill of rocks below, deposited by cascading runoff waters in the past. The river, viewed so close, seemed to move with a life of its own, grumbling and sighing against the rocky shore. The surface seethed, a brown maelstrom pockmarked with whirlpools that appeared suddenly, writhed past, and then disappeared again as though pulled under by a giant hand.

Shaun picked up a large stone and heaved it down one of the swirling pools. The stone fell with a loud *chunk,* displacing a crown of spray that splattered back into the water to be immediately re-absorbed. Bethany shuddered at the relentless power of that deep pulsing current. She reached one hand toward Bobby in a protective gesture, wanting to hold onto him but knowing he'd resent it if she did. Following Shaun's example, the boy selected a rock and threw it as far as his thin arm could propel it, laughing when it produced a *kerplop* sound, not so loud as Shaun's stone had created, but obviously satisfying to the child.

They threw rocks for several minutes, trying to make the flat ones skip over the current. Then Bobby looked around for something else to do and Bethany saw his face light up when his gaze fell on the old rowboat tied to the jetty.

"Let's go out in that," he said, pointing with the fingers of his right hand, still pale from being concealed inside the cast.

"No, honey, that's too dangerous," Bethany protested.

The thought of Bobby in a boat out on that treacherous river caused a sour taste to rise inside her throat. She wanted to keep him safe from any further hurt . . . ever—although she knew such a wish was unrealistic—all children must encounter bumps and scrapes during their childhoods, even in families where there is no abuse.

But Shaun echoed her concern when he said, "Not a good idea, sport. In the first place, that boat is too small for three people, and in the second place we'd need a motor out in that current or else we'd be swept downstream and wouldn't be able to get back. You go out in that, son, and you might wind up drifting clear to the Mississippi and on down to New Orleans!"

"Just like Huck Finn did?" Bobby asked, his face glowing with obvious pleasure at the idea.

Oh no! Bethany thought. *Maybe I've poured it on too thick about Huck Finn.*

The events of the next few minutes convinced her of it. Before she could react to what was happening, Bobby took off at a run toward the weather-beaten pier attached to the jetty. He darted over the blackened boards and jumped into the boat, which slipped from its precarious perch against the slimy rocks to the edge out into the water. Although the boat was still tied to the jetty, Bethany saw it wobble with the slap of the waves. That was just enough to throw

Bobby off balance, toppling him headfirst into the mud brown water. Bethany let out a shriek of terror.

Shaun was already sprinting over the pier in pursuit of the child. Now Bethany saw him quickly pull off both shoes and dive at a flat angle off the end of the pier. When he, too, disappeared beneath the current, Bethany felt her breath freeze in her chest. For one moment she almost collapsed with the weakness in her knees. Then she inhaled deeply, willing strength back into her body.

Grabbing up a long leafless branch from a pile of flood debris and racing along the edge of the water, she kept her eyes fixed desperately on the surface of the river as she watched for the two heads to reappear. Bobby popped up first, sputtering and flailing, and then Shaun surfaced nearby, searching frantically in all directions for the child.

"There he is!" Bethany shouted. "Shaun, to your left!"

Shaun lunged in that direction with arms and legs beating through the water as though driven by an engine. Bobby went under again and Shaun dived after him. Bethany strained to find them in the murky water. Beyond, further out toward the middle, she saw another whirlpool form.

Oh, God, please, please, don't let them get caught in that! she pleaded.

She started to strip off her own shoes to go in after them when Shaun emerged again, with Bobby clutched under one arm. She saw him try to strike out for shore, but the weight of the child, combined with the force of the current, worked against him. Bethany looked down river and saw a sand bar about a hundred yards away, projecting out into the water.

"Shaun, there's a sand bar just ahead! Swim at an angle toward shore," she shouted, waving both arms to get his attention. "The sand bar! Swim for the sand bar!"

When she saw that he understood, she sprinted away over the rough rocks, still clutching the tree branch, and ran out onto the pebbled bar to try to grab the two of them as they floated by. She saw them coming, rolling along like a flood-tossed log, with Shaun fighting to keep Bobby's head above water while kicking his feet in a frantic effort to break free of the current that threatened to sweep him out around the end of the bar and on down the river.

"Grab the branch! The branch, Shaun, grab it!" she screamed, then flung herself down on her stomach on the end of the bar and dug her toes into the sand, while extending the branch as far as it would reach out over the water.

As Shaun swept by, he struggled to grasp the branch with clawed fingers. For one heart-stoppng moment, Bethany thought he was going to miss it; but he gave one frantic lunge and latched on, holding so tight that his knuckles paled to ivory. Pulling with all her might, Bethany scuttled backward over the bar. Soon Shaun lay gasping on the sand, while Bobby coughed and gagged nearby. When Bethany found that they were uninjured, she repeated like a litany, "Thank You, thank You, thank You," in tearful gratitude that their lives had been spared.

"Quick thinking, B.C.," Shaun murmured as he pulled her close for a cold wet embrace, then extended an arm to include Bobby. The three of them held each other while Bethany thanked God once more for saving her family.

But they aren't your family, whispered the nagging inner voice. *Shaun is not your husband, and Bobby has a mother who will one day take him back.*

If she could just believe that Shaun loved her . . . but such happiness still seemed so elusive even as the branch, moments before, had seemed for a time to be beyond Shaun's reach as well. She felt dizzy, as though she were being carried along by currents of emotion as powerful and overwhelming as the rumbling river. Could people actually drown in such emotion? If the pounding of her heart and the choking in her chest were any indication, then she had to admit that such a thing was a possibility.

Lord, help me, she cried in silent supplication, but the lines of communication that had been open when she prayed for Shaun and Bobby now seemed closed to her. She clung to the two of them as to a life raft.

CHAPTER 8

BETHANY HAD WORRIED THAT SHAUN and Bobby might suffer delayed consequences from their narrow escape, but other than a few bruises and skinned places, they proved to be just fine. In fact, when Bethany returned to the hospital on Monday evening to work on the mural, she learned that his friends had declared Bobby a "hero."

That evening, and each evening thereafter throughout the week, while he and Bethany worked on filling in the big areas of the mural with basic colors, he talked about the good time he'd had.

"Can we go again? Can we go again soon?" he kept begging.

Her heart turned over as she looked down into his eager face. She didn't want to deny him anything—especially when it took so little to make him happy.

"Maybe, honey. I'll ask Dr. Rosselli."

Her heart gave a second lurch as she remembered

Shaun's breathless kiss after their tumble down the grassy slope, the feel of his arms hard about her . . .

But when she suggested another outing to Shaun, he acted in an unpredictable manner that stung her feelings.

"It might not be such a good thing right now," he said cooly. "We're really working hard to bring about a reconciliation between Bobby and his mother, and I don't want to do anything to upset the apple cart."

"What do you mean? How could another picnic possibly hurt?" She knew she sounded accusatory, but she honestly couldn't understand how giving Bobby another happy time would affect his relationship with his mother.

Shaun gave her a long hard look. "I'm not thinking of Bobby. I'm thinking of you."

"Me?"

"Yes. Bethany, you're growing too fond of the boy. Of course, that's *my* fault. I brought the two of you together. Believe me, I know it's hard not to let your feelings run away with you when it comes to these kids, but you just can't let yourself become too involved. You have to remain objective if you can. Bobby is not yours, he's not mine—he *will* be going back to his mother, and *soon*, now that his arm is healed. I do want the two of you to finish this mural, because this has been a positive experience for him. But be prepared for the fact that he'll be going out of your life one of these days."

And you—will you be going out of my life, too? Are you warning me not to get too involved with you, either? Bethany thought bleakly, staring up at his stern face.

Nausea gripped her and for one brief moment the

room wavered before her eyes. Shaun was thirty years old—how many women had he known in his life, women with whom he hadn't wished to become too "involved?" Was she just another in a steady stream of them—some, patients whom he counseled—like Bobby's mother; others, temporary companions to fill idle hours? And how did he view her—counselor or colleague? More importantly, when their work together was done, would he tell her goodbye?

Bethany was still brooding when she got home that evening. She carried her mail into the apartment and began absently thumbing through it, then stopped with a shock of surprise when she saw the logo of her old advertising firm in the corner of a long gray envelope. When she removed the letter inside, she found that it was from Lyle Thomas, the man she'd described so uncharitably to Shaun the previous weekend as being "short, bald and probably in debt." The letter proved that she had misjudged his financial condition. Things were going very well for him, he told her—so well, in fact, that he'd opened a second branch of his firm in St. Louis, and he wanted her to come back to supervise her art department there.

"I've always admired your work," he wrote, *"and now that you've gained new experience working for King, I think you'd be a valuable asset to my firm. Please let me know if you're interested."*

He then proposed a salary that caused her to gasp—it was over a third again as much as she currently received.

She stood staring down at the letter for a long moment without moving. Here, handed to her on the proverbial silver platter, was the perfect way out of her dilemma. She could accept Lyle's offer and leave this town, away from Bobby, away from Shaun. . . .

She swallowed against the sudden ache in her throat at the thought. Desolation poured through her like a gray fog. Never to touch Shaun again, never to look into the blue wonder of his eyes—but he himself had warned her against getting too involved. Better to break it off now, rather than risk even greater hurt. With an opportunity like this for advancement in her career, she had a logical excuse for walking out of Shaun Churchill Rosselli's life—just as he had warned her that Bobby would soon walk out of her life, and, by inference, that he would, too.

She carefully put the letter away in the top drawer of her desk to ponder a little longer. It was possible she had misunderstood Shaun's intent when he'd said she shouldn't get too involved. Surely he hadn't meant she should be prepared to give up her friendship with him, too. . . .

But on Saturday she decided he had indeed meant to include himself in that warning. It happened after she and Bobby had finished filling in the last large area of the mural with its base coat of paint. The panorama now looked like a magnified page from a coloring book, with its pale blue sky, white clouds, tan tree trunks, pearl gray water, figures patterned in flat colors. Looking like a "paint by number" kind of design at this point, it was now ready for Bethany to go back and put in the shading and details. But even in that simple form, the mural had life and energy. Bethany felt proud of it and of Bobby's part in the project so far. She bragged on him enthusiastically in front of Shaun, and hugged the boy close before he was led off by the nurse to go back to the children's ward.

Later, when Shaun walked with her to the parking lot, he said flatly, "You didn't listen to me the other day. I warned you about getting too attached to Bobby—"

His patronizing tone set her teeth on edge.

"What's the matter, don't you think I can handle this?" she asked.

"It's just that the project will end soon. I can tell you're building up false expectations for the future—that, deep inside, you expect things to continue as they are—It won't happen—it can't, Bethany."

So she was right. He had been warning her about their personal relationship. A pain stabbed through her heart, as sharp as though she'd been wounded by a sword.

"Have you become a mindreader?" she parried lightly.

"No, but some of the signals I've picked up from you worry me."

Suddenly all of the frustration and doubt Bethany had felt for the past few days came pouring out in anger. "Who do you think you are, telling me what to do? You psychologists—you're all alike! Cold and calculating, playing with other people's heads. Well, I don't like it, not one bit!"

"Hey, wait a minute—"

"*You* wait a minute. You think you have all the answers. Well, maybe you don't. How do you know what Bobby really needs, what *I* need . . . "

"What *do* you need, Bethany—do *you* know?"

His voice carried an edge she'd never heard before, slicing across her nerves.

"That mystery about you I sensed at the first, that touch of sadness that made me notice you—well, we've been together for many weeks now, and I'm beginning to figure out more about you than you think."

He grabbed her wrist and held it out between them so that the scars gleamed like a silvery web in the parking lot light.

"I've asked you about this before, but you've never answered. Who did this to you? Your mother, your father? From the way you've reacted to Bobby's mother, I'd bet it was your mother. Is she the hooded figure in that painting you have on your wall at home?"

Bethany jerked with shock at his perception. How could he have guessed . . . .

"Let me go!"

"Not until you tell me. Get it out, Bethany, don't suppress your emotions—"

At that, anger blazed through her body like the eruption of a forest fire. "How dare you pry into my life! You have no right to do that, no right at all! I'm not your patient."

She tried to pull her arm away, but he held on to her firmly.

"I'm your friend, Bethany. That gives me the right—"

"No, it doesn't. My life is my own, and I don't have to share it with you, or with anyone."

He gave her wrist a little shake. "Your mother or your father, Bethany? which one?"

"My father's dead," she burst out. "A long time ago."

"How old were you when he died?"

"Ten. I was ten. . . ." She paused, feeling her heart squeeze with grief as she tried to picture her father, now little more than a shadowy figure in her mind, scarcely more than a vague silhouette, but tall and strong, nonetheless. "He was wonderful, my father. My Mom and I both adored him. . . ."

When she stopped struggling, Shaun let go but kept his eyes glued to her face. Bethany lifted her hand to rub her forehead, feeling puzzled by her last statement. Was it true? Had her mother ever actually adored anyone? But she had a sudden vision of happier days—a time when her parents were embracing, saying loving words. . . .

"How did he die?" Shaun's voice, still flat and holding no emotion, probed insistently.

"A car wreck. He was alone that night, and he fell asleep at the wheel. That's what the police said later. He'd wanted Mom to go with him to a church meeting, but I'd had a cold so she stayed home with me—"

A dim memory stirred in the back of Bethany's mind—elusive, fleeting. The memory vanished to be replaced by her mother's anguished voice lashing out at her after the police had brought the news: "If only I'd been with him. If I hadn't stayed home with you. . . ."

Shaun's voice interrupted the flashback in Bethany's mind: "What happened afterward?"

Bethany blinked as she came back from her vision of the past to see Shaun still fixing her with a look that probed her brain like a scalpel. Resentment toward him flared in a heated wave.

"See, that's what I mean about you scientists. You don't care who's hurt so long as you can carry out

117

your experiments. Because that's all I am to you, isn't it, just an experiment, a specimen to be dissected? Is this how you treat all your patients? If it is, then I don't think I like you very much."

She whirled and ran for her car, wanting to get away from him and those cold eyes, once so gentle but now frozen into ice, as blue and forbidding as a glacier. She knew she would not return to the hospital, not after that outburst. The board would have to find another artist to help Bobby finish the mural. As for Lyle's offer—she'd be a fool to turn down all that money. She'd write to him tomorrow accepting his offer, thereby putting Dr. Shaun Churchill Rosselli out of her life—once and for all.

CHAPTER 9

UPON REFLECTION. BETHANY saw that she'd have to get more answers from Lyle before handing in her notice at King, such as when the new office in St. Louis would be open for business. She could not afford a six month delay before starting her new job.

Bethany wrote to Lyle telling him that she was very interested and that she'd appreciate more information. But realizing that a good job was waiting for her in the wings gave her the courage to face a second fact: She could not walk out on the hospital and leave her job unfinished. Although she no longer believed, as she had as a child, that God was watching and judging every action, she still felt a strong moral obligation to complete the project as agreed.

But if Dr. Rosselli thought she should remain detached, then that's exactly what she would be. When she next encountered him in the hallway at the hospital, she spoke to him in a polite but cool voice that could have frosted corn.

He cocked one eyebrow in a quizzical way. "Bethany, about the other day . . . "

"Don't worry about it," she replied, giving him a light smile. "Bobby and I almost have the mural finished. I'll soon be out of your hair."

The casual cliché, uttered by Bethany without thinking, gave her a sudden pang as she looked at Shaun's black locks spilling about his head in careless profusion. She found herself wanting to reach out now and brush them back from his broad forehead that had furrowed slightly at her last remark.

"I've tried to call you several times but you weren't home," he said.

She'd let the phone ring each time, suspecting who it was.

"Well, yes, I've been very busy lately," she commented. "There's a chance I may take a new job in St. Louis."

His face paled. "What—"

"But don't worry," she put in quickly. "I won't leave until the mural is finished. And now, Bobby's waiting. . . ."

She hurried away briskly, not looking back to see how he had taken her news. She hoped it had given him at least one brief moment of pain, although she suspected that he had the science of detachment down pat.

With Bobby she was also matter-of-fact, no longer taking time out to tell him stories.

"Dr. Rosselli wants us to get this finished, so we'd better work hard," she explained in a no nonsense voice. "Here, shade in the leaves on this bush the way I showed you last time."

"Bethany," Bobby asked in a small voice, "are you mad at me?"

"No, of course not," she replied, wanting to hug him, but restraining herself. "It's just that our paints and brushes have been cluttering the cafeteria long enough. We need to finish quickly now, so people can eat their lunches in peace."

"When we get done, what will happen? You'll still come to see me, won't you?"

"Oh, I'm sure I will, once in a while; but you'll be going home soon, Bobby. And this fall you'll start school again—"

"But I want to go on another picnic. Please, Bethany, can we go? Can we go tomorrow?"

"No, Bobby, we can't!" Her words popped out in an exasperation born of her own unhappiness. "Just get to work, okay?"

She stroked one side of a tree trunk with her brush, darkening the edge to give a three-dimensional effect. When she sensed no activity going on beside her, she turned to see Bobby curled up on the floor in a fetal position, his brush clutched tightly in one fist. Quickly she knelt beside him and touched his shoulder.

"What's the matter?"

When he didn't answer, she took hold of his head with both hands and turned his face to see tears squeezing from the corners of his eyes.

"You don't like me anymore."

The despair in his voice filled her with remorse. So much for detachment, she thought wryly. She gathered him up in her arms and rocked him back and forth with her face buried in his hair.

"Of course I like you. I could never stop liking you . . ."

"Bethany!"

Shaun's exclamation cut off her crooning as effectively as a slammed door. She glanced up to see him frowning down at her in disapproval. She glared back defiantly. If he couldn't see that this child needed reassurance, then he wasn't much of a psychologist.

"Just taking a little break," she remarked casually while daring him with her eyes to question her further. Then to the child, she said, "Look, Dr. Shaun is here! You want to show him the leaves you've just painted?"

Bobby stirred and sat up, rubbing the back of one hand across his cheek to wipe away the tears. The paint on the brush he was clutching left a swipe of green on his face. Wordlessly he pointed toward a clump of foliage beside the water.

"Looking good!" Shaun said with a false enthusiasm for the boy, but the glance he flung toward Bethany was forbidding.

"Bobby also helped me put in the shading on the raft. And, here, these reflections in the water—these are his," she said brightly. "And the dog on the bank—Bobby did almost all of that. He also put in the shading on Huck Finn's hat, and there in the field, that horse . . . "

"You're both doing a good job," Shaun replied. "It's causing a lot of comment throughout the whole hospital."

"Can we paint another picture when this one is done?" Bobby asked, sudden hope lighting his face.

"Not another mural," Bethany told him quietly, "but you may still paint pictures of your own. I'll give you a set of water colors and a large pad of water color paper—"

"—and I'll come and live with you and we'll paint together," Bobby chimed in.

Bethany's stomach lurched at his words. She was drawn against her will to glance toward Shaun who flashed her a look that said, as loudly as though he had spoken audibly, *See? I told you so.*

"No, you'll be going back to your own home soon," Bethany told him, "but we'll still be friends, Bobby."

"Forever and ever?"

"Yes, forever and ever."

Seemingly satisfied for the moment, Bobby went back to work on the leaves. Bethany locked eyes with Shaun while murmuring in a low voice, "There, was that better, doctor?"

"Bethany, we've got to talk—"

"I think it's all been said, don't you?"

"No, I don't. When you're through here, stop by my office, okay?"

"I need to get home—"

"Please, Bethany. You can't drop a bombshell saying you may move, and then not explain."

The appeal in his voice could not be denied. The ice had melted from his eyes, replaced by a look that might be grief—but she wasn't sure. Curiosity alone would have compelled her to accept his invitation. But later as she and Bobby cleaned up for the evening, she found that there might be a chance with Shaun after all—

You're a dreamer, she told herself, cutting off the speculation. *He's curious about you, too, and that's the size of it. But to think he's in love with you? Come off it, Bethany, you know better—no one is ever going to fall in love with a mixed-up person like you.*

Nevertheless, she found herself breathing faster in anticipation when she entered his office. She'd stepped inside his reception room a couple of times before, but this was the first time she'd ever seen the actual inner sanctuary where he worked with patients on a one-to-one basis.

She'd expected to find the severe desk and black leather couch that seemed to be synonymous with movie psychiatrists, and was, therefore, pleasantly surprised to find the room a warm homey place. There was thick tan carpet, a couch, a loveseat and chair upholstered in a beige nubby fabric with brown and tan pillows, and hanging plants in beaded macrame holders. A table sat in one corner with magazines and toys, and bright abstract paintings adorned the walls. Among those was Bobby's poster paint design, glowing like a jewel inside a wide tan mat and brown frame.

Shaun had been standing beside a window staring out into the darkness. Now he turned to face her. "Please sit down, Bethany," he said politely, pointing toward the couch while he came to sit opposite her in the chair.

Instantly she was on guard. This was too much like a setup for a counseling session.

"Nice room," she remarked to cover her reaction. "Did you decorate this yourself?"

"Yes." But he sounded distracted, studying her face as though he were trying to pick up clues. She remembered he'd said that psychologists watch for signals in their patients, so she deliberately smoothed out her expression, keeping it as blank as possible.

"Bobby's painting looks lovely in that frame. Has he seen it?"

"Yes, we meet here three times a week."

"What does his mother think of it?"

"You're stalling, Bethany. What did you mean when you said you may move to St. Louis?"

124

The suddenness of his approach took her by surprise. She felt her hackles rise.

"Just that. Lyle—that's Lyle Thomas, my old boss—has offered me a job in the new branch of his firm. I'd be in charge of the art shop, supervising several other artists in illustration and layout work. It's a great opportunity—"

"Bald-headed Lyle—the one in debt?"

"That's the one. Although he seems to be doing very well, after all."

"Are you taking the offer?"

"I may."

"So you're running away."

He made the statement simply, in a casual tone that took a moment to sink into Bethany's consciousness; but when it did, she once more flared with anger.

"What do you mean, running away?"

"Isn't that what you're doing? You're running way from me, but most of all you're running away from yourself—"

She came to her feet, indignation flaming her cheeks.

"I did not come here to be analyzed!"

"Ah, you're angry. That's good." He said it with an analytical coldness that fired her even more.

"Don't use that tone of voice with me!"

"Something is eating away at you, something you've kept hidden for a long time. You need to talk about it and get it out of your system. I *am* your friend, Bethany. Trust me. Nothing you could say would shock me—"

"Oh, really?" she asked in a scathing tone. "What about a mother who pours boiling water over her daughter's wrist and hand?"

The minute the words were out, she clapped her

hand over her mouth, shocked that she had uttered aloud a secret she'd suppressed for years.

"Is that what happened?" Shaun spoke without sympathy, as though she'd just commented on the weather.

"Isn't that enough?"

"I've heard worse. Did she do it on purpose?"

Bethany's pulse pounded in her throat. The old aching fear, the insecurity she'd felt as a child, washed over her in a choking wave.

"She said it was an accident—"

"But you don't believe that."

"I've read there are no such things as accidents—that an accident is really a subconscious wish to hurt or to be hurt."

"Your father died in an accident—"

"My fault! It was my fault!" The confession burst from Bethany in an agonized gasp.

"How?"

"If I hadn't been sick . . . if Mom had gone with him instead of staying with me . . ."

"Then they both might have died. Bethany, you can't accept that kind of blame."

"*Mom* always blamed me for it."

"Did she?"

"Afterward, she changed, became more withdrawn . . . strange. I don't know how to explain it, but she didn't seem to like me anymore. Sometimes she'd be so mean, it was as though she'd become someone else, similar to those evil stepmothers in the old fairy tales. Then other times, she'd make over me and say she loved me. I never knew what to expect. . . ."

"That's a typical pattern in child abuse."

"Well, I hate her, and I hate God for allowing

126

something like that to happen—to Bobby or to me. He has to be cruel and vengeful—"

"God is *not* like that, Bethany," Shaun interrupted. "*People* may sometimes be cruel and vengeful, but most of them don't want to be that way, and they hate themselves more than anyone else could possibly hate them for the things they do. I believe that most people are basically good and, if they behave in an ugly way, they're usually crying out for help. That's why I got into this business—to try to help people deal with their emotional disabilities, so they can learn to live together in love and harmony. That is the heart of Jesus' whole message—that we should love and help one another. I know you well enough by now to know that you are indeed a loving woman. If you feel you hate your mother, then there's a reason for that . . . "

"See? You are trying to psychoanalyze me!"

Tears stung Bethany's eyelids, tears that she insisted were due to anger. Underneath, she suspected that Shaun's words had struck a responsive chord she didn't want to recognize. Little mice of doubt raced about in her head as she tried to hold on to her rage against her mother, mice that whispered that there had been many happy times, too. . . .

"No, I'm just trying to be your friend," Shaun said in a soothing tone. "You're hurting, Bethany. If you'd just talk about it—"

"I don't want to talk about it—to you or to anyone else!"

"Sooner or later you'll have to come to terms with this, B.C., or it will continue to poison your life. Your mother undoubtedly had some serious emotional problems that were triggered by your father's death: problems of coping, problems of her own guilt over his death that she took out on you. But I'll bet she loved you, Bethany, more than you know. How long has it been since you've seen her?''

''Almost a year.''

''Have you written to her?''

''No. But she hasn't written to me, either. I did hear from my aunt a few months back, saying that Mom was sick at that time, but I put off answering—''

She waited for his condemnation of her negligence. He said nothing but continued to watch her with a concerned look on his face that she decided must be his professional expression.

''When we had our last blowup a year ago, she said she never wanted to see me again,'' she went on. ''I took her at her word.''

''Sometimes people don't say what they really mean. She may have sent you away because she felt that's what *you* wanted. She may really have been wishing for you to reassure her and say you wanted to stay.''

''That's absurd!''

''Not really. If you could just forgive her, Bethany—you'd see. . . .''

''Forgive her? All I want to do is get out of this town and go somewhere else where I can start over and forget about the past.''

''You can't run away, Bethany,'' Shaun said quietly. ''No matter where you go, this problem will follow you until you look at it squarely and learn to deal with it. I want to help you, if you'll let me.''

For a moment she was tempted. But the anger had been a part of her for so long that she found she could not let go that easily. It was as though she were clinging to it in vindication of her own actions, her own neglect of her mother for the past year. If her mother were really sick . . .

It was too much to think about; her head had begun to ache and now she pressed the base of her palm against her forehead.

"I really have to go, Shaun. Thank you anyway."

She snatched up her purse and exited without looking back. She'd thought he might follow to walk her to her car, as he usually did; but this time he let her go alone.

Oh, God, why don't You just reach down and make everything right in this world? she cried as she stumbled through the parking lot.

She wanted to hold out her hand and have Him take it, proving to her once and for all that He was really there. She opened her car and climbed inside, then fumbled about in the zippered side of her purse for a small paper bag, now wrinkled and soft with wear. She pulled out the sand dollar and turned on the overhead light to read the legend: *. . . The five slits around the edge represent the five wounds in the body of Christ . . . on the top of the shell is an Easter lily . . . break open the shell and you will release five small white doves, messengers from God to spread Good Will and Peace to all Mankind.*

She felt a yearning in her heart for that promised peace, yet some perversity in her nature denied her the right to ask for it. At last she put the shell back in her purse and headed her car out into the night.

CHAPTER 10

FOR THE NEXT TWO EVENINGS Bethany worked alone on the mural so that she could move swiftly without having to stop every few minutes to explain things to Bobby. She wanted to finish the painting and get away from the hospital, once and for all.

On Friday, when she returned to her apartment, she found a letter from Lyle. In it he said that the St. Louis office would be ready to open in four weeks and that he would appreciate an answer from her as soon as possible. She resolved then to call him on Monday to accept his offer. That way, she could give the King Company two weeks' notice and have an additional two weeks to settle her affairs, find an apartment in St. Louis and pack for the move.

With the decision finally made, she expected to feel relieved. Instead, she had a hollow feeling in the very middle of her being, as though she were a tree without a core. She looked at the twisted tree in her painting and thought, *Hollow trees blow down in storms.*

She studied the other symbols in the painting—the rose, the key—what had they meant to her when she'd first painted them? She was no longer sure, although she knew that the rose had sometimes, in painting and in literature, symbolized Mary, the mother of Jesus. That made her think of the bas relief of the Madonna and Child in Chandler Court where she and Shaun had gone on the first day they met. The memory of that day came back with a rush—the feel of the damp air, the tangy taste of the grapes, her first dizzying descent into the blue depths of Shaun's eyes.

And the golden key, what was that? The key to the solution of her problems? Had she been hoping subconsciously for such a key even then when she'd first painted the picture? Shaun, she suspected, would probably tell her that the key to release the pain that bound her spirit was forgiveness.

She paced the floor, unable to contain the uneasiness that possessed her. At last she went back out and drove through the warm summer night with all the windows down, hoping that the soft air would soothe her jangled thoughts. As though drawn by some invisible force, she found herself slowly circling through the streets of the Country Club Plaza. All the shops were still open and brightly lighted, while the fountains glittered like geysering fireworks under the glow of the street lamps. When she passed Chandler Court, she was startled to see a man with black curly hair leaning close to a blond woman at one of the tables. For one brief moment she felt she was looking into a time warp, that the two people were herself and Shaun.

The drive only served to disturb her more. She finally went home to bed, where she tossed restlessly all night, haunted by dreams that fled as soon as she awakened in the morning, but left her feeling drained, as though she had put in a hard night's work.

Her face, when she put on her make-up, looked haggard and drawn. She brushed her hair until it stood out about her head in a filmy cloud and re-applied her eye shadow and lip gloss, attempting to hide the telltale lines of fatigue before heading for the hospital one last time. There were only a few small spots left to be touched up on the mural, perhaps an hour's work, no more.

She'd hoped to avoid Shaun, but he was the first person she saw as soon as she entered the lobby. He drew her to one side.

"We've got a problem. Bobby's mother showed up early this morning for a joint counseling session with Bobby, and she came unglued and tried to attack him before I could get her calmed down. It's really shaken him up, Bethany. I know you don't really need him anymore on the mural, but could you find *something* for him to do, something that will take his mind off what just happened?"

She'd tried to harden herself against Bobby, preparing herself for the separation soon to come, but her heart went out to him once more as Shaun described the scene with his mother.

"Of course," she said. "One of the things left to do is to sign our names to the mural, and I want his to be first, above mine."

Shaun's face brightened. "That will be a thrill. Our annual open House for all the hospital benefactors comes up in three weeks—and I'd like to have an unveiling of the mural, with a special party for Bobby and the other children from his ward." He searched her face for a long moment. "You will be here won't you? You're not really going to move to St. Louis, are you?"

"I'll be in St. Louis, Shaun. My new job starts in four weeks."

He held her eyes for a long moment while his brows lifted in a look of dismay. He distractedly pushed his curls back from his forehead, leaving them in a tangled disarray.

"I thought maybe you'd change your mind," he said bleakly.

She plastered a bright smile on her face as she replied, "It really is an excellent opportunity for me. To be in charge of an art shop—well, that opens all kinds of doors, could maybe even lead to the owning of my own advertising firm someday."

"Is that what you want?"

Looking at him, she felt her joints weaken as she thought, *No, Shaun Churchill Rosselli, I want you.*

For one wild moment she was tempted to say just that; but what if he should put on his "professional face" and reply in an impersonal voice, "That's very interesting. Shall we discuss the meaning behind this strange impulse?"

Instead, she said, "Of course. It's what I've worked for for years, through my training in school, my jobs with Lyle and at King. I'd be a fool to pass it up."

"Yes, I guess you would. I'll miss you."

Such a common thing, such a *safe* thing for him to say. No histrionics, no pleading. *Which shows,* she thought, *that his feelings for me aren't too deep or he'd come up with a stronger reply.*

She excused herself and hurried off to the cafeteria.

Several people were having their mid morning coffee, but they just glanced toward her in casual curiosity before going back to their conversations.

She put on her smock, spread a canvas drop cloth on the floor in front of the mural and then arranged the paints and brushes on a small table nearby. She stepped back and examined the whole painting with a critical eye, noting the areas that needed to be touched up or emphasized before setting to work. A stroke of titanium white here to show sunlight on a ripple, a splash of burnt umber there to strengthen a shadow. Small additions, but important ones, soon gave the painting an added zest that it had lacked before.

When she stepped back a second time to study the whole effect, she heard a spattering of applause and looked around to see the coffee drinkers clapping and nodding their heads in approval. She smiled and bowed slightly to acknowledge their tribute. A nurse brought Bobby in just at that moment, and Bethany gestured toward him while saying to the people at large, "This is Bobby, who also helped paint this mural. How about a hand for him, too?"

The people responded with even greater enthusiasm, but Bobby looked startled and confused by their attention and turned to hide his face against the nurse. Bethany went to get him and led him gently across the room, away from the others, to stand before the mural.

"Look Bobby. You really *did* help do this. What do you think of it?"

He peered up through coppery lashes to examine the mural.

"I think it's pretty," he announced at last.

135

"You know what we're going to do now?" Bethany asked, and then answered her own question: "We're going to sign our names here in the right-hand corner where everyone can see. That way, all the people who come here from now on will know that Bobby Ryan is one of the artists who painted this mural."

As the coffee drinkers rose to leave the cafeteria, a female visitor approached them. "I think it's wonderful what you people are doing here in this hospital for these children."

She reached out and briefly touched Bobby's shoulder before turning to follow her friends. The nurse waved and left, too, calling, "I'll be back pretty soon. Just take your time."

That left the cafeteria empty, except for the cashier over by the food section and a couple of servers chatting by the door leading into the kitchen, which suited Bethany just fine. She felt sad, now that the last session with Bobby had finally come, knowing that soon she would be moving away and that Bobby would indeed walk out of her life. She wanted these last few minutes to be private and special—just the two of them finishing together the project they'd worked on for so long.

She helped Bobby load a narrow brush with brown paint and let him practice writing his name on a large piece of paper before leading him to the mural and showing him again where to sign. Working with great concentration, the tip of his tongue protruding from the corner of his mouth, Bobby carefully painted in his name. When he finished, Bethany took the brush from him, dipped it into the can of paint, and then added her name below his.

"There! All done!" she announced. "Oh, Bobby, aren't you proud?"

His eyes shone as he slowly scanned the mural. "I painted that dog."

His voice held wonder, without a note of bragging, as though he wanted to seal the reality of his accomplishment by saying it aloud.

"And that horse—and that bird—and there, those bushes," Bethany said, pointing to the various areas.

Bobby's thin shoulders straightened with pride. "Dr. Shaun says we're going to have a party. Will it be like the picnic? Will we go to the river, just you and me and Dr. Shaun?"

"No, I think that party is going to be here," Bethany told him, "and all your friends will get to come. Lots of grownup people will be here, too, and they'll all be looking at the painting. They'll see your name and know you helped paint this—"

"And your name, too."

"And my name, too."

"And you'll be here for the party and then we'll paint some more pictures," the boy rambled on, his eyes shining with the dream, "because we're friends, forever and ever. You said so."

Bethany realized, with a sinking in the pit of her stomach, that she was going to have to explain to Bobby that she was moving to St. Louis and would miss the party. For one brief moment she was tempted not to say anything. It would be so much easier just to disappear quietly from his life; but that would be the coward's way out, and deceitful, too. To let him go on believing something that wasn't true would be the same as actually telling him a lie, and Bobby deserved better from her than that.

She knelt down beside him and placed her hand on his arm. "Yes, Bobby, I am your friend, and I always will be; but sometimes friends have to be separated for a while. Sometimes they move away from each other and can't get together as often as they'd like, but that doesn't mean they aren't still friends."

Bobby's face creased with a puzzled frown. "I'm not moving away."

"Well, you might, when you go back with your mother—"

At the look of fear and dismay on Bobby's face, Bethany paused, wanting to bite her tongue as she remembered what Shaun had said about the scene that morning between Bobby and his mother.

"No," cried Bobby, "I don't want to live with her; I want to live with *you*. I want *you* to be my mother."

He flung his thin arms around her and buried his face against her neck. Bethany felt her heart contract with grief. She realized that her words to Bobby the other day about going back with his own mother hadn't sunk in, after all. All this time, even as she'd been fantasizing about building a family around Bobby, he had been dreaming the same thing. Shaun was right. She'd made a mistake in building up false hopes in this child as well in herself by not keeping her objectivity. She'd have to set him straight at once. She put her hands against his shoulders and pushed him away, holding him at arms' length.

"Now listen to me, Bobby, listen carefully. I do love you, but I'm not your mother, and you can't come to live with me. Dr. Shaun is working with your mother, and she's getting better, Bobby. She really is. Dr. Shaun says so. Soon you'll be able to live happily together."

Oh, dear God, let them live happily together.

"But I want to live with *you,* " he repeated against her neck. "You won't ever leave me, will you?"

"Honey, I have my own life to live, too. I won't forget you, that's a promise. But I'm moving soon to St. Louis—"

He stiffened and pulled away from her grip. "You already promised we'd be friends forever and ever."

"We will be. Just because I live somewhere else—"

"You *promised!* " His face had turned so pale that his freckles fanned across his face like a splash of dark stars against a white sky. The accusation in his eyes burned into Bethany like the touch of a red-hot iron.

"Bobby, try to understand. I've been offered a good job in St. Louis . . . "

A feeble excuse, she told herself. *Children don't understand about jobs.*

"When?" he demanded.

"When am I leaving Kansas City? Soon. I'll have to find an apartment and move my belongings—"

"Don't go, please don't go." His voice was little more than a whisper, but the plea was unmistakable. Bethany retreated from the misery on his face, telling herself, *He's not your problem. Shaun will just have to deal with this himself at their next session.*

Further argument seemed pointless; the best move would probably be to distract him, to get his mind on something else.

She stood up and said in a soothing voice, "I know this seems confusing, but someday you'll understand. Come on now, honey, we need to get this mess cleaned up. You bring these brushes, and I'll carry these rags, and we'll go to the janitor's closet and use his sink . . . "

She turned away, busying herself with the task of gathering up the rags and rolling them into a bundle. She heard a scrambling noise behind her, a small grunt of exertion, and turned just in time to see Bobby fling brown paint across the center of the mural. The whole center of the painting disappeared under the spreading ugly splash that flowed downward like brown blood, oozing, dripping, a terrible wound in the middle of what had just moments before been loveliness. Bethany stood, stunned into immobility by the sight, but Bobby flung himself forward and attacked the painting with his bare hands, spreading the paint in both directions with a frenzied sweep of his arms. *Swipe*, and his dog's legs disappeared under the avalanche of muddy brown; *swish*, and Huck Finn's head was gone; *splash, splat* . . .

Bethany darted forward and attempted to grab Bobby's arms, but he eluded her grasp like a slippery fish while continuing his destructive attack. A thin wail came from his throat, like the cry of a mortally wounded animal. It was a chilling sound, the sound of total despair.

"Bobby, please!"

Using all her strength, Bethany gripped his shoulders and dragged him away from the mural. He twisted about in her hands and attacked her now with the same energy he'd used against the mural, kicking her shins and beating against her with his fists.

"Let go of me!" he screamed. "I hate you! I hate you!"

The cashier, noticing the struggle, hurried over and tried to catch hold of the hysterical boy, but to no avail. As Bethany leaned forward to wrap her arms around him in an effort to calm him, he hauled back one paint-smeared hand and slapped her hard across the face. Before she realized what she was doing, she slapped him back, an exchange of blows that stopped him as effectively as a brick wall. He stared up at her, his eyes wide, his mouth frozen open in shock. Then with a sigh, he slid to the floor and curled up once again in the fetal position, with his eyes tightly closed and his arms folded over his chest. After the noise of the past few minutes, the sudden silence pressed against Bethany's skin like cold pudding.

"Oh, my God," she whispered, her words not an oath but a plea, a spontaneous calling out, in this moment of crisis, for help. She knelt beside Bobby and took him gently by the shoulders. "Bobby, are you all right?"

He lay as unresponsive as a windup toy that had run down. His eyes remained closed.

"Bobby, please—"

When he still did not respond, she turned to the cashier. "Send someone to get Dr. Rosselli."

The woman nodded and hurried away while Bethany sat down on the floor and gathered Bobby up in her arms. His paint-smeared hands were clenched in tight fists against his chest; his breathing ragged. She rocked him, staring bleakly at the damaged mural.

What have I done? Dear God, what have I done? she cried in silence, her body trembling as she held the child. She couldn't believe she had actually struck him. She recoiled from the dreadful admission. To strike a sick child, a child who had already been abused by another woman he'd thought he could trust . . . She laid one cheek against his hair, the enormity of her crime so horrifying to her that she couldn't

141

even cry, although her throat stung and her eyes burned.

Shaun arrived on the run. She saw him flash a startled glance toward the paint-smeared mural before dropping to his knees beside her and Bobby.

"What happened?"

"I tried to explain I was leaving. He seemed okay, but then— I don't know, he just went crazy, and now—" Her voice broke and she swallowed hard before continuing. "Now, he's like this. Shaun, I didn't mean . . . ."

But Shaun had already taken the boy from her. He rose and stretched Bobby out on one of the tables, taking his pulse, listening to his heart, thumbing up one eyelid to look into the brown orb that stared back without recognition. Bethany's own heart skipped wildly about in her chest.

"Oh, Shaun, he's not—"

"—dead? No, of course not. But he is in shock. Tell me again what happened."

Stumbling over words, gulping for breath, Bethany related the whole sordid episode, holding nothing back about her own complicity.

"I hit him, Shaun. I can't believe it, but I did!"

"All right, I'll get him to Emergency. Call the emergency desk to say we're on our way, then see what you can do here," Shaun said brusquely, jerking his head toward the mess on the wall. "Wait for me. I want to talk with you as soon as Bobby comes out of this."

He gathered up the boy in his arms and strode rapidly toward the door. Shaking as though she were coatless in a winter blast, Bethany hurried to call Emergency on the house phone near the register while the cashier, cooks and servers clustered nearby, talking among themselves and glancing in dismay at the mural.

After Bethany finished the call, she leaned her aching head against her fisted hands, wishing she could erase the last half hour and start over. How could she have done such a thing—how could she have hit Bobby! The accusing question echoed over and over in her mind. She wanted to rush down to Emergency to check on his condition, but the harsh sound of Shaun's last command held her back: "See what you can do here," he had said. And then he had told her to wait.

She got two fistfuls of paper napkins from the serving line and dragged herself back over to the mural where she first used rags to blot the wet brown paint from the wall, then went back over the ruined areas with the napkins, sponging, wiping, doing the best she could to minimize the damage. The cafeteria workers tried to help her by bringing paper towels from the restroom, along with a bucket of water; but when some diners came in for early lunch, the others had to go back to their regular duties, leaving Bethany to struggle alone as she scrubbed up trickles of paint that had spilled down onto the floor. Repairs to the painting itself would take a major effort. She felt sick when she looked at Bobby's dog, now legless under the swipe of brown. He'd been so proud of that dog. . . .

She threw away the dirty rags, wadded clumps of paper and the empty can of paint before carrying the other supplies out to the trunk of her car. She wanted desperately to know how Bobby was doing, but she felt sick at the thought of facing Shaun again after the awful thing she had done. He would despise her now, even as she despised herself. There was nothing more she could do for Bobby. She had quite effectively done it all, she told herself, feeling cold desolation envelop her.

After reaching home, she paced the floor as she relived the awful scene in the cafeteria. On one of her turns, she caught sight of her painting with the dead tree, the rose and the key. The painting seemed to issue a silent reproach. She took the painting off its hook and stood it with its face against the wall.

CHAPTER 11

"Is BOBBY THERE?"

Shaun's curt question caught Bethany by surprise. When the phone had rung, she'd picked it up with shaking hands, steeling herself for news of Bobby's condition and Shaun's condemnation. To be asked if Bobby was with her was the last thing she'd expected.

"Isn't he with you?"

"No. He's either hiding or he's run away."

The fear in Shaun's voice struck a responsive chill in Bethany's own body.

"How can that be! He wasn't even moving—"

"When the shock wore off, he switched into an opposite kind of behavior—got very agitated, very wild. He's horrified over what he's done—"

"Over what *he's* done?" she interrupted. "I'm the one . . ."

"Don't be too hard on yourself. He'd lost control and had to be stopped."

"But I slapped him—"

145

Shaun didn't seem to hear her as he hurried on with his report: "Bobby's distraught over what he did to the mural. He knows he's ruined it, and he's afraid you won't love him anymore."

Bobby—gone . . .

A black pit seemed to yawn at Bethany's feet.

"You think he's headed here?"

"I don't know. He was only at your place the one time, so I don't know how he'd ever find you. There's no telling where he's gone."

Bethany remembered when she'd protested about the locked doors at the hospital and how Shaun had asked her to imagine a sick child lost in the woods surrounding the grounds. As she pictured Bobby stumbling along through the tangled undergrowth, not watching out for snakes or poison ivy, his freckled face swollen with crying, she felt fear clench her heart.

"Have you called the police?"

"Yes. They've put out a citywide alert and are getting ready to launch a search now in the woods. Hospital personnel are out looking for him, too, and we're still searching the hospital just in case he's holed up somewhere inside."

The sheer weight of her guilt made Bethany's knees begin to buckle. "If I hadn't told him I was leaving— or maybe if I'd said it in a different way . . ."

"No time for that. What we must do first is find him," Shaun reminded her flatly as he cut in across her words. "Look, I have to go. The police are waiting for me."

After he hung up, Bethany sank down on a nearby chair and buried her face in her hands. Memories from her own childhood flickered past in rapid succession, and she felt again the way she'd felt when her mother, so loving one minute, would fly suddenly into a rage: Small Bethany had reasoned that it *had* to be her own fault. She was a bad girl or her mother wouldn't act that way. Rejection, the worst pain of all, was proof that love is not deserved. And now she had "rejected" Bobby by telling him she was leaving.

You're ugly, she now told herself with loathing. *Ugly and mean.*

Bethany sat suddenly rigid in her chair, electrified by a new thought: Could her own mother have ever felt this way after one of her scenes with Bethany? Could she have been overwhelmed by this same kind of remorse . . . ?

Unable to sit still any longer, Bethany asked her neighbor to watch her apartment in case Bobby showed up and then headed for the hospital to help with the search. As she drove, her mind raced about in circles like a trapped animal, trying to figure out what Bobby was thinking and feeling at this moment, where he might have gone. The scenery passed in a blur at the periphery of her vision while she stared at the road, driving without conscious volition, responding automatically to the traffic.

Then a portion of the scene ahead suddenly came clear, as though it had been spotlighted to get her attention. She saw a steeple rising sharply above the trees, like a pointing finger, a summoning beacon that drew her forward as a magnet draws iron. As she traveled farther, the church came into view—a large, tan, stone edifice with stained glass windows. She felt a sudden compulsion to stop and go in. The rational part of her mind argued that such a thing didn't make sense, that she was needed in the search at the hospital. Nevertheless, her hands displaying a will of their own, turned the steering wheel and edged the car into the parking lot.

Maybe I'm supposed to pray for Bobby here, she thought, directing her steps toward the vestibule. She wondered what she would do if the church proved to be locked, but the door swung open at her touch, admitting her into the cool dimness of the outer lobby. She crossed the dark green carpet and pushed open the doors leading into the sanctuary.

The windows, jeweled paintings outlined in traceries of lead, admitted beams of colored light that fell upon the pews like a blessing. Bethany gasped, awed at the sight, her artist's sensibilities touched by the glowing splendor. She advanced down the aisle, walking as softly as she could, not wanting to disturb in any way the sense of peace that permeated the very air. She was still feeling puzzled by the impulse that had brought her here.

Then she stopped, frozen to the spot by the sight of a window more powerful, more beautiful, that any she had ever viewed in her life. The grouping showed Jesus on a hillside with his arms around several children. The words below, scripted in gold, read: *Suffer little children, and forbid them not, to come unto me: for of such is the kingdom of heaven.— Matthew 19:14.*

This Jesus was not the delicate blond man portrayed by many artists, but strong and powerful, with broad shoulders and a lean jawed face. His brown hair blew back from his face, as though a brisk wind swept up the hillside. The robe he wore looked rough and homespun. His extended hands were large and calloused, the hands of a carpenter used to hard work, or of a fisherman who had hauled in many a heavy net. But his gesture, as he embraced the children, was gentle, and the look in his eyes held love so all-emcompassing that Bethany felt physically touched, as though she were actually a part of that circle of children.

Jesus, we don't know where Bobby is, but You do.

The thought came to her with blinding surety, like a burst of light. She went to her knees in the aisle and buried her face in her hands against the side of the pew.

"Oh, God, please, please, keep Your arms around him, don't let him go. Stay with Him, Lord, wherever he is . . ."

A picture floated into her mind, coalesced, as real as a photograph. It was a picture of a small redhaired boy in a rowboat in the middle of a brown rolling river.

The vision brought her to her feet, her eyes open now as she looked, startled, toward the altar.

"The river, he's on the river," she whispered, her body sweeping with chill. For she knew it was true as surely as though she'd heard the message spoken aloud. She and Bobby had often stood at the windows of the cafeteria and looked out over the trees toward the river while she told him the Mark Twain stories. It was only a mile away through those woods, no hike at all for a nine year old.

Thank You, Lord, she prayed. *Please, keep him safe until we can get there.*

She turned and hurried up the aisle, anxious now to find Shaun and give him the news. She felt certain he would trust her vision, but she wasn't sure how the police would react. They might dismiss her as some kind of religious nut.

"I'll just have to convince them," she told herself firmly.

When she arrived at the hospital, she saw a police car parked near the edge of the grounds leading into the woods. An officer seated inside was talking over a radio mike. Bethany parked and hurried over to him, saying, as he turned off the mike and looked questioningly toward her, "Do you know Dr. Rosselli? Is he around here anywhere?"

"The doc?" He gestured toward the woods. "Yeah, he went off with Joe. They're in there somewhere."

Bethany pulled her brows together and chewed her lower lip as she looked at the shadowed timber laced together by thick undergrowth. She could wander around in there for hours and not find him.

"Can you call Joe on that radio?"

"Yeah, he's got a hand held."

"Would you call him and say that Bethany knows where Bobby is, and she needs to get hold of Dr. Rosselli?"

The officer's face lighted with excitement. "Lady, do you really know where that kid has gone?"

"He's in a rowboat out on the river."

The man's eyes bugged and he gaped at her in disbelief. "How do you know that?"

"A reliable source," she stated with conviction, thinking, *The most reliable source there is*.

He questioned her no further, but got on the radio at once. Over the buzz of static, he spoke with someone whose voice sounded tinny and far away. The voice then changed, and another, almost unrecognizable because of the distortion, said, "Bethany, are you there?"

The officer handed her the mike and showed her how to press the buttons.

"Yes, Shaun, this is Bethany."

"You say Bobby's on the river?"

"Yes."

"How—"

"Just trust me, will you? I'm in the hospital parking lot—"

"I'll be right there," he interrupted in a rush, and the radio clicked off.

Bethany paced nervously until Shaun came bursting from the undergrowth, his shirt soaked with perspiration, his hair a hopeless tangle about his tense face. He was followed by an officer Bethany assumed was Joe, a man who also showed signs of rough travel through the woods. They both came pounding up to Bethany, to be joined by the officer from the car.

"Did someone call you about him? Did you see him yourself?" Joe queried when they reached her.

"Well, in a way, yes." Bethany paused, her eyes begging Shaun to believe her. "Shaun, I stopped at a church to pray, and I asked God to show me where Bobby was. I had a vision of him in a boat on the river—"

Joe made a gesture of disgust. "Oh brother!" he muttered, turning away.

But Shaun kept his eyes riveted on her face. "You saw him—"

"As clear as a photograph, well, more like an actual film of him moving down the river. He's there! I know he is!"

Shaun turned to the officers. "We'll shift the search to the river—" But Joe shook his head while the other officer viewed Bethany with a skeptical look on his face.

"If we followed the lead of every nut who comes to us with information, we'd never get anything done,"

151

Joe stated flatly. "There's no way we'll call in our men because of some dame's 'vision.'"

Shaun looked at them both for a moment, then seemed to realize the futility of further argument. With an air of dismissal, he turned to Bethany. "Let's take my car. I don't know how fast that current flows, or where he found a boat. There's no telling how far—"

"Doc, do you really believe her?" the first officer asked in surprise.

"Absolutely! It's exactly the kind of thing Bobby would do." He took Bethany's arm. "Come on, let's hurry."

As they headed for Shaun's car, Bethany heard one of the officers mutter, "I always knew psychologists were crazy."

"So much for my reputation as a 'clinical scientist,'" Shaun murmured.

They drove to the nearest through street and headed for the river as fast as the speed laws would permit.

"If we had a police escort, we could go faster," Shaun remarked with a trace of bitterness in his voice.

"I knew they wouldn't believe me," Bethany told him gently, "but I'm glad *you* did. I was praying for that."

Shaun reached out one hand and she held it briefly before releasing him to tend once more to his driving. She felt confident and hopeful of finding Bobby soon; but when they reached one of the long lacy bridges that tied the southern and northern halves of Kansas City together, her spirits fell. Though she strained her eyes to scan the twisting expanse of the river, she saw no sign of a child in a rowboat.

"How will we find him?" she cried in despair.

"While we drive around through this traffic trying to get to another bridge, he could fall out of that boat, or float on by." She watched a light plane take off from the old municipal airport next to the river. "If we were in a plane or a helicopter—"

"Good idea," Shaun said quickly. "Let's see if we can rent one."

He wheeled the car into a side street and headed for the airport. Once the site of all of Kansas City's air traffic, the location had been abandoned many years before by the major airlines in favor of a larger jetport out in the country. Bethany could understand, for the runways here were not long enough to accommodate the big jetliners. The light plane business, however, seemed to be thriving. Colorful rows of single-engine and twin-engine planes lined the parking areas.

Shaun parked in front of the office, and he and Bethany both jumped out to hurry inside. Shifting impatiently from one foot to the other, they waited in line behind a short wiry pilot, who seemed to have an endless list of questions for the man behind the desk. When at last he was satisfied, he headed off down a side corridor while the desk clerk asked Shaun, "What can I do for you?"

Quickly Shaun outlined the problem.

"We don't have a helicopter pilot available right now," the man told them, "but that fellow who was here ahead of you, does charter work, and he just landed in his Cessna. It's out there now, being refueled. He might be willing to go back up and fly you over the river."

Shaun grabbed Bethany's hand and they took off at a run down the corridor after the man in the flight suit. They caught him just as he left the terminal building.

Panting for breath, Shaun repeated the story.

153

"We'll pay you for your time and the rental of the plane," he concluded.

A frown creased the man's forehead. "Listen, I'd like to help you—I've got a kid of my own. But have you looked over there?"

He pointed toward the southwest. Bethany glanced in that direction and saw a line of dark clouds rolling in toward the city. Although the sky overhead was still blue, she knew that soon the wind would begin to rise.

Bobby, out on that river in a storm . . . the thought caused ice to form around her lungs.

"Look, just twenty minutes—could you take us up for twenty minutes?" Shaun asked.

The man turned to scan the darkening sky, then said hesitantly, "It will take a least ten to fifteen minutes just to get back into the air," he said at last, "but I figure we have forty-five minutes before the weather gets really bad. Let's go for it!"

He paid the driver of the fuel truck, then called back over his shoulder, "By the way, my name is Chuck," as he strode purposefully toward a blue and white single engine place. Pointing to the ropes that stretched from the wings to rings embedded in the asphalt, he said, "Okay, you two, untie it while I check it out."

Shaun and Bethany set to work at once while the pilot felt the edges of the wings, the tail, the propeller, jiggling this, peering into that, until he pronounced the plane ready to fly. Bethany climbed into the back seat and fastened her shoulder harness. Shaun took the front right-hand seat next to Chuck, who was checking a lengthy instrument list and throwing switches on the control panel. Bethany chewed her thumbnail with anxiety at the delay.

At last Chuck opened the window on his side of the plane and yelled, "Clear!"

He turned on the ignition and the engine roared to life, causing the propeller to disappear in a whirling blur. After talking with the control tower, he taxied to the end of one of the runways where he revved the engine again while re-checking his gauges and dials. Finally he wheeled to the center of the runway and pointed the nose down the center line. Slowly the plane began to roll, hugging the ground until, at the climactic moment, Bethany felt the little plane lift and soar into the air.

"You okay?" Shaun asked, glancing back over his shoulder.

Bethany nodded, then directed her attention out the window. Soon they were over the river and she looked down at the writhing current.

"How fast does this river flow, do you know?" Shaun yelled to the pilot above the roar of the engine.

"No idea. Looks pretty fast, out toward the middle." Flying low, they passed over a barge, and Bethany's heart skipped with hope when she spotted a small boat up ahead; but it proved to be a motorboat carrying a couple of fishermen.

"If we only knew when and where he got that boat," Shaun shouted over his shoulder to Bethany.

"That would help, all right," she called back.

She hadn't realized how much debris the river carried. A floating log gave her a start before she realized what it was. The shifting patterns in light and dark caused by wind riffles and cloud shadows on the surface of the water sometimes made details hard to distinguish.

"Over there!" Shaun called excitedly, pointing toward the right. But when the pilot banked the plane in that direction and Bethany peered down, she heard a groan from Shaun that she echoed when she saw that the boat once more held a fisherman.

They crossed another bridge, and then another, and still there was no sign of a rowboat carrying a small boy.

"Could he have landed somewhere by now?" Bethany called to Shaun.

"I doubt he'd try that. Remember how excited he was at the thought of going all the way to New Orleans?"

Bethany nodded bleakly. She glanced toward the storm and saw that rain was already falling over the southwestern edge of the city. The plane rocked, struck by a gust of wind.

"Getting bumpy," the pilot observed. "We'll have to turn back soon."

"Just a little longer," Bethany pleaded.

Down below the waves were beginning to kick up in the rising wind. If the boat tipped over and Bobby drowned, Bethany knew her life would be over, too, for she'd never by able to forgive herself.

Please, Jesus, keep him safe, she begged, trying to hold in her mind a picture of Bobby surrounded by Christ's love and filled with His light; but her fear kept getting in the way.

Then she saw a dark speck far ahead, bobbing on the waves.

At the same time Shaun pointed, shouting, "There! Is that a boat?"

"Looks like it," the pilot said as he dipped lower over the water.

Bethany kept her eyes glued to that speck, watching it grow larger and resolve into a rowboat holding one figure. A small figure.

"It's Bobby!" Shaun yelled, his voice breaking with excitement. "Can you call the field and ask them to notify the police?"

Chuck nodded, "I know what bridge he's headed toward. I'll ask for squad cars and the police helicopter."

While Chuck talked over the radio, Shaun glanced once more toward Bethany and she saw him grin for the first time since they'd begun the search.

"Can you imagine how this news is going to affect our friend Joe and his buddy?" he asked.

A warm fizzy feeling rose inside her, like bubbles in a carbonated drink, and she smiled, too, thinking of the two men's upcoming surprise and chagrin. Then she sobered. The battle wasn't won yet—not until they could get Bobby safely to shore.

They flew low over the rowboat and soared on down river. Shaun tapped Chuck on the shoulder while motioning toward a dirt road that ran through a long vacant field toward an old boat landing. A car and boat trailer were parked nearby.

"There's a motorboat down there putting in toward shore. Maybe we could get that fisherman to take us out to Bobby," he said. "Could you set us down in that road?"

Chuck gave a wry laugh. "Might get me in trouble with the authorities, but I'll claim this was an emergency. Just let me check on the wind direction."

He circled around, peering down at the trees in a nearby field and at the fluttering flag atop an official looking brick building in the next block.

"If I don't land into the wind, we'll flip over," he explained.

He lowered the flaps and sank toward the field while Bethany held tightly to the edges of her seat.

The plane touched down hard, bounced up again, then landed once more and jarred along over ruts and rocks.

"Not the best landing I ever made," Chuck apologized.

"Good enough," Shaun told him.

As soon as the plane stopped, Shaun unlatched his seat belt and gave Chuck a business card. "Here's my office number. I'll get back to you with payment."

"Don't worry about it, just save that kid," Chuck replied roughly. "I have to head for the airport now before that storm gets any closer."

"Right."

Shaun crawled out, then turned and helped Bethany down. They set off at a run toward the dock, their clothes whipping in the wind. Bethany heard the roar of the plane and glanced back to see the Cessna race down the field and lift into the air. The wings wobbled a couple of times, but Chuck managed to keep the plane under control as he headed into the darkening sky.

"I hope he'll be okay," she said when Shaun looked over his shoulder toward the disappearing plane.

"He'll make it," Shaun reassured her. "Come on, let's catch that boat."

They began waving and yelling to get the fisherman's attention. He waved back, and Bethany could see that he was indeed headed in their direction. They darted down the sloping landing to meet him. An ominous rumble of thunder echoed over the water, reverberated, slowly died, followed several seconds later by a flicker of lightning. Bethany rose on tiptoe to nervously look back up the river toward the drifting speck that was Bobby's boat.

"Hi, there!" the fisherman hailed when he drew closer to shore. "You wanna give me a hand?"

He lifted a coil of rope and tossed one end toward Shaun who caught it and then scrambled frantically to keep from slipping into the water. Bethany grabbed his arm and held on until he could regain his balance while the fisherman cut the motor and drifted in to bump against the landing.

"Actually we want *your* help," Shaun told him. "There's a nine year old child about to float past us in a rowboat, and we have to get him off this river before the storm hits."

The man's face grew grim at the news. "Oh, boy."

He turned and looked toward the city where the skyline had now vanished under a curtain a dark rain. Overhead, fast-flying gray cloud streamers heralded the rising wind.

"I just came off this river because of that storm," he continued. "Do you know how easy a small boat like mine can swamp when those waves get rough?"

"Yes," Shaun said, "but you've got a motor and he hasn't. He'll never make it alone."

Bethany had tried to quell her fears in order to function, but Shaun's words made the danger real again. A spurt of gall burned her throat and she swallowed painfully.

"Please," she begged. "We can't let him drown!"

The man took a deep breath, then set his mouth in a tight line of determination. "Come on!"

The boat rocked as Bethany climbed in and settled herself in the center seat. Shaun cast off, then splashed into the water and scrambled aboard.

"All set?" the man asked. "I'm gonna run it full throttle, so hang on."

He started the engine and guided the boat back out

into the current where wind-frothed waves chopped against the boat like angry fists. Spray drenched Bethany's arms as she held onto the sides.

"Gettin' ugly!" the man called above the roar of the wind and the engine. "There are flotation belts— there on the bottom of the boat! Put 'em on!"

Shaun handed Bethany one of the belts—a bulky thing that wrapped around the chest and fastened with Velcro. As she slipped into it she thought about Bobby, so small and defenseless, out there with no protection.

Jesus, You're his only chance, she whispered desperately. *You were out once in a boat in a storm— You and Your disciples. Even Peter was scared, Lord, remember? Bobby is just a little boy. . . .*

The rain struck then, a cold sweeping blast that drummed against the surface of the river in a deafening roar.

"Do you see him?" Shaun yelled.

Bethany peered into the gauzy curtains of water, trying to make out one small tossing boat, but all she could see were the churning waves.

"No . . . wait a minute, is that it?"

She pointed into the wind toward something dark that bobbed up, disappeared into a trough between waves, then bobbed up again. It was a rowboat, all right; but it was empty. At the sight, a cramping pain gripped Bethany's stomach and she bent over, clutching herself and breathing hard against the blackness that threatened to engulf her.

He can't be gone, he can't, not after all this! she cried silently. *Lord, You wouldn't have let go of him, surely not!*

"He's in the boat!" Shaun yelled.

Bethany lifted her head. Her vision was fuzzy, and

it took her a moment to focus. Then she saw, as they drew nearer, that Bobby was huddled in a tight ball on the bottom of the boat, his arms over his head against the rain.

Thank You, oh thank You, she breathed, weak with relief.

"Easy now," the fisherman advised. "We don't want to tip him over with our wake."

He throttled back and edged up to Bobby's boat while Shaun called, "Bobby, it's Dr. Shaun. We've come to get you, son. You'll be all right now."

Bobby lifted his head. He seemed not to know, at first, what was going on, or who they were. His eyes looked as big as an owl's; his wet hair plastered about his head and his soaked shirt clung to his slight frame. Bethany could see he was shivering. When he started to stand up, Shaun called, "No, son, stay where you are. I'll get you."

Both Bethany and the fisherman grabbed hold of the side of Bobby's boat and held on to keep it from drifting away while Shaun stripped off his life belt, then leaned over and fastened it around the boy. He grabbed him under the arms, holding tight as he dragged him over the side of the smaller boat and into their own. He handed the boy to Bethany who held him close, trying to warm his shaking body.

"Bobby, Bobby, Bobby," she whispered as she stroked his wet hair back from his face. She kissed his forehead, her tears mingling with the rain.

"It was all my fault," she told him. "My fault, not yours. Don't worry, we can fix the painting—it isn't ruined. I wouldn't hurt you, honey, not for the world. Please, please forgive me."

Time seemed to stop and she waited in a swirling chaos for his reaction. Then his arms crept around her neck and he sighed with his head against her shoulder as though he'd been relieved of a great burden. Bethany, too, felt a dark weight lift from her spirit.

He's forgiven me! she thought, her heart singing with joy. Tears spilled from her eyes now in an unrestrained flow.

Forgiveness, the greatest gift of all.

That's why Christ died for us on the cross, she thought in awe.

She'd never known before what that really meant. To be forgiven. What a blessed, blessed thing.

Bethany stopped, struck by a sudden knowledge: Her mother was suffering, too, suffering from that same dark weight that had, until a few moments ago, pressed so heavily upon Bethany. She knew now, with a conviction that brooked no argument, that she must get home as soon as possible to offer her mother that same chance for peace that Bobby had just given her.

Forgiveness.

"Thank You, Lord," she murmured with her face pressed against Bobby's cheek. "Thank you for Your love that forgives us—and helps us to forgive."

CHAPTER 12

BETHANY PARKED HER CAR at the curb in front of the small wooden house where she'd grown up, a house she hadn't seen since that fateful day over a year ago when she had gotten into an argument with her mother during a visit.

"Leave!" her mother had said then. "I don't want to see you anymore!"

And Bethany had done just that.

Well, Mom, I'm back she thought, gripping the steering wheel with the need to hang onto something solid. *How are you going to feel when I walk through that door?*

She hadn't phoned to say she was coming. Shaun had thought maybe she should, but she feared if she did and her mother acted hostile, she might lose her nerve.

What nerve? she chided herself ruefully. *Here you sit, afraid to go in.*

The house looked more run-down than she remem-

163

bered—with peeling paint, a broken gutter, and last autumn's dead weeds still in the yard, sticking up like scarecrows above the struggling grass. When her father had been alive, he'd taken pride in the yard, she remembered, planting borders of flowers along the sidewalks and keeping the grass trimmed like a plush green carpet. The old catalpa tree, there in the corner, had held her rope swing, a swing her father had tested every year to make sure that it was still safe. He'd replaced that rope whenever it showed the slightest signs of wear, she remembered with a smile, saying when he did so, "I don't want my little girl to get hurt."

And her mother in those early years had made her a whole family of rag dolls with lots of clothes. . . .

She leaned her forehead against the steering wheel and closed her eyes. She couldn't put if off any longer. She would have to go in.

"All right, Lord, I'm here because of you," she said quietly. "You're going to have to walk in there with me because I can't do it alone."

Bethany straightened and reached for her purse, then opened the door and climbed out. Her feet felt encased in lead as she dragged herself up the sidewalk to the front door. Her pulse began to race, and she took several deep breaths, willing herself to calm down before ringing the bell. Such a long time went by that she began to fear no one was home. Then she heard footsteps, a fumbling at the doorknob, and the door opened to reveal the surprised face of her Aunt Jean, lean jawed and sallow under a crown of limp gray hair. But the smile that dawned on the old woman's face was like sunrise overcoming the night, casting a flush of beauty over features that had, just moments before, appeared plain.

"Bethany! Oh, Bethany, you've come!"

Aunt Jean stumbled through the open doorway in her eagerness, and Bethany reached out to catch and steady her. The woman seemed to see that as an invitation to an embrace, for she extended her arms, too, and enfolded her niece in a tight hug. After a moment, she pulled away and took off her glasses, wiping them carefully on the edge of her apron. Then she fitted the stems back over her ears.

"Just let me look at you. I can't believe you're really here."

Bethany gave a shaky laugh. "I can't believe it, either, but here I am."

"Oh, honey, it's been so long."

"Yes, I know. Is . . . " She paused to steady her voice. "Is Mom here?"

Her aunt studied her face. "Did you get my letter?"

"Yes, you said Mom had been sick—some kind of tests . . . "

"Bethany, she has cancer."

The news hit Bethany like a blow. "How bad is it?"

"Pretty bad. She's taking treatments, of course, but she's not responding well. I don't know, she just doesn't seem to have the will to live."

Bethany felt strength drain from her body and she stood for a moment with her head drooping against her chest. She'd thought, from her aunt's letter, that her mother might have arthritis or something, but she hadn't been prepared for this.

Finally she straightened. "May I see her?"

Her aunt nodded, stepping aside to let Bethany enter.

"She's in her old bedroom down at the end of the hall."

Bethany's nose was assailed by odors as soon as she stepped into the dark hallway. Her aunt must be cooking stew, she thought, for there was a steamy feel to the air, a soup smell, vegetables and meat simmering together. But there were other odors less pleasant—the smell of disinfectant—which could not mask the pervading sour smell of sickness. She heard her aunt shut the door and sensed her hovering presence behind her in the hall, but she focused her attention on one door ahead that stood ajar, the door leading into her mother's bedroom.

"I'll just let you go on in alone," her aunt murmured. "If you need me, I'll be in the kitchen."

"Okay, thanks."

Bethany paused beside the door and clenched both hands for a moment to stop their trembling. Then she pushed open the door and stepped inside. The sick smell hung like a pall in the room, dark because of the closed draperies. She had to wait for her eyes to adjust before she could make out the form of her mother lying very still in the old brass bed under a thin summer quilt. When she crept closer, she could see that her mother was asleep. The sunken cheeks and translucent blue eyelids, the wasted arms lying motionless on top of the cover, revealed how ill she truly was.

Bethany pulled up a straight-backed wooden rocking chair and sat down next to the bed. She studied the sleeping woman's face, the wispy hair, almost white now. When she'd seen her mother last, her hair had still been brown with only a few gray streaks. Then she cast her eyes about the bedroom, re-acquainting herself with the cream colored wallpaper sprigged with tan flowers, the heavy oak dresser with its marble top and oval mirror that hung suspended in the middle of a lyre shaped support.

Her eyes stopped there, and she caught her breath on a slight gasp of surprise when she saw one of her old rag dolls sitting on top of the dresser. She rose quietly and tiptoed across the room. It was the doll her mother had designed to look like Bethany when she was six years old, with a pug nose and long blond pigtails. Its dress was of the same blue checked material her mother had used in making Bethany's dress to wear on her first day of school. Bethany's eyes filled with tears. She took the doll and hugged it close, and carried it back to the bedside where she sat down and gently rocked back and forth. The last time she'd seen that doll, it had been stashed in the old trunk in her own room, along with the "Mama" and "Papa" dolls her mother had created when she'd made the "Little Girl." Her mother would have had to have dug it out on purpose, or have asked Aunt Jean to do so. More than anything else her mother could have done, the gesture spoke to Bethany of loneliness, of a desire to recapture a time when their world had been happy and warm.

She looked at the little rag doll once more. The resemblance to herself at the age of six was unmistakable. Her mother had been a true artist, she realized, although she'd taken those talents for granted when she'd been young.

And it was her mother who had encouraged her, during the calm rational periods, by saying, "Take that money your father left you and go to college,

167

Bethany. Get your art degree, make something of yourself. You're got the talent, you can do it.''

So different from those other times when in a rage, her mother would lash out and say, ''You're worthless, you'll never amount to anything.''

You were just like that old poem, Mama, she thought now, *that old nursery rhyme about the girl with the curl in the middle of her forehead. When you were good, you were very very good, and when you were bad, you were horrid.*

''Be prepared,'' Shaun had warned her when she'd told him of her plan to go home. ''She has a definite emotional problem. But it's good you're going, Bethany, because you'll never be free, no matter how far you run, until you come to some kind of understanding with her. Do you want me to go with you?''

She'd been grateful for his offer, but preferred to face the situation alone.

''Just call my supervisor for me at work, will you, and explain I've gone home to handle a family emergency?'' she'd asked.

So here she was, back in Clear Springs only two days after Bobby's rescue. She could hardly believe how fast her life was moving. But looking at her mother's tired face, she knew she'd been right to come home, no matter what reaction she encountered.

She leaned forward and lightly clasped her mother's hand. The woman stirred and emitted a soft moan, little more than a sigh. Her eyelids flickered, then opened halfway, and she stared blankly toward Bethany for a moment. Then recognition dawned and her eyes flew wide. Her mouth worked, but no sound emerged. She turned with a visible effort and clung to

Bethany's wrist with her hand, hanging on as Bethany had clung to the steering wheel. The appeal on her face was so naked, so grief stricken, that Bethany could hardly bear it. She slid from the chair and knelt beside the bed, gathering the frail woman close.

"Mama, I'm home."

The woman's thin arms came up to encircle Bethany's neck. Her voice, when she spoke, was a reedy whisper. "I've been praying you'd come."

Her mother held onto her for a long moment, and Bethany listened with dismay to her labored breathing. Then her mother sank back against the pillow.

"Are you all right, Bethy?"

Her mother's old pet name, used when her daughter had been very small, made Bethany's heart swell.

"Yes, Mama, I'm fine now."

"Can you . . . " The woman's voice broke and she took several shallow breaths before continuing. "Can you forgive me?"

"I already have. And I want you to forgive me, too."

In answer, the woman once more held out her hand and Bethany clasped it between both of her own. She stroked it gently until her mother fell asleep.

"Is she going to make it?" Bethany later asked as she sat in the kitchen with her aunt as the older woman arranged a bowl of soup and a cup of tea on a tray.

"That all depends," her aunt replied. "The treatments seem to be zapping the cancer, but the doctor says she's got to want to live. I've known for a long time that something was eating at her besides that cancer, that things weren't right between the two of you. Cassie always was nervous, even when she was a girl. And after Jim was killed in that wreck, well . . ."

Bethany nodded at her aunt's unfinished sentence. "So there *is* a chance—"

Her aunt threw her a sudden smile. "There's always a chance, don't you know? With you back again . . . well, honey, I think it's going to make a world of difference."

Bethany stood up and placed a folded napkin on the tray beside the bowl of soup.

"I'll take her supper to her, if that's okay."

"You bet it's okay."

This time Bethany pushed open her mother's door with eagerness instead of fear. She found that her mother had switched on the lamp beside the night stand and was sitting up, propped against a pillow.

"You know something? I'm feeling better," her mother said. Her voice was still weary, but she managed a smile. "I think I'll be able to eat tonight. Lately, I just haven't had much appetite."

Bethany carefully extended the legs on the tray and place it across her mother's lap, then sat down once more in the rocking chair. She kept the conversation casual while her mother ate, telling her about her job at King and describing all the beautiful fountains in Kansas City.

When her mother finished, she took the tray and placed it on the dresser. Her mother stirred restlessly and Bethany turned to see once more that look of appeal on her mother's face.

"There's something I have to say," her mother began in a hesitant tone. "I—I've always loved you. I don't know why I acted so hateful sometimes . . ."

"Shhh," Bethany murmured, walking back to the bed.

"No, I have to say this. I can't rest until I do. When your father died—well, he and I had had an argument that evening . . . "

The memory of it came back to Bethany in a sudden flash. *That* was what had nagged at the back of her mind, the scene she couldn't quite recall.

"He'd wanted me to—to get a sitter for you and go to church with him, but I was still sulking and I used your cold as an excuse to stay home."

Her mother paused and closed her eyes for a moment as though gathering the strength to go on. Bethany felt she should say something soothing to stop what was obviously a painful confession, yet she felt a compulsion to hear her mother out.

"When the police came . . . and said he'd fallen asleep at the wheel, I . . . just couldn't face it. He'd died before we could forgive each other. It was a burden I couldn't bear. I kept thinking if only I'd gone with him . . . so I tried to blame you for it, instead. Can you—can you possibly understand . . . ?"

Bethany felt tears sting her eyelids. If Bobby had drowned before she had made things right with him, she would never have forgiven herself.

Forgiveness.

She remembered that old adage, *Don't let the sun go down on your anger.*

"Mama, I do understand, I really do, but I'm sorry its taken me such a long time. What we must do now is love each other and go on."

"Just hearing you say that—well, now I can die in peace."

"We're going to work together toward getting you

171

well," Bethany said firmly. "Here, Mama, I want to show you something."

She got her purse from the night stand and rummaged around until she found the small wrinkled blue sack.

"This is a gift from a friend of mine," she went on when she had found the sand dollar. She took out the fragile white shell and laid it in her mother's hand. "Have you ever heard the legend of the sand dollar?"

When her mother shook her head, Bethany said, "Listen and I'll read it to you."

Her mother turned the shell over and over in her hands, looking at the cross, the flower, the indentations, while Bethany read the story from the card. Her face had begun to glow with a kind of inner light by the time Bethany finished.

"That's beautiful," she whispered reverently, rubbing her fingers over the shell.

"I want you to keep this sand dollar and the card with the legend here beside the bed, and every day you're to concentrate on God's healing love," Bethany told her.

"In that drawer—a long pink ribbon . . . ," her mother replied, pointing toward the dresser.

Bethany found the ribbon and brought it back to the bed. With shaking fingers, her mother carefully threaded the ribbon through one of the holes.

"Would you tie this around my neck?" she asked.

Bethany gently lifted the wispy strands of her mother's hair and knotted the ribbon so that the shell, holding its secret cache of tiny white doves, lay like a locket on her mother's breast.

"Thank you, Bethany," her mother murmured, her

eyes shining with renewed life. "Thank you for everything."

Again, Bethany rocked quietly and chatted with her mother about the happy times until the frail woman, looking rested and peaceful, dozed off with her fingers lightly clasped about the shell.

CHAPTER 13

BETHANY CHEWED THE END OF HER PENCIL as she checked over the grocery list. A slight frown marred the usual smooth expanse of her brow. Then her expression cleared and she snapped the fingers of her left hand.

"I know what it was—Mom asked for mint tea."

"Oh, that's right, I'd forgotten." The older woman turned from the stove, wiping her hands on her flowered apron.

Bethany added tea to her list, then glanced up and caught her aunt staring at her with an expression that seemed almost shy.

"You've done her a world of good, coming here like this," the woman said softly. "I see a peace in her now I haven't seen in a long time."

Bethany felt tears sting behind her eyelids. "I'm the one it's helped, more than you'll ever know. I—I understand now why some of those things happened

175

between us. It's too bad I couldn't have realized sooner."

"The important thing is, you *did* come, and you got here in time. Thank God for that . . . "

"Thank God, indeed!" Bethany echoed fervently, adding silently, *Oh, yes, God, thank You . . . thank You for never forsaking me, even when I thought You weren't there. Thank You for placing forgiveness in my heart. Put Your arms around my mother, Lord, keep her warm with Your love. . . .*

A yearning to see Shaun suddenly swept over her like a sudden gust of warm wind. She wished she could tell him everything that had happened, share with him the wonderful healing that forgiveness brings, just as he had told her it would. Maybe she would phone him after supper. Just the thought of hearing his voice once more made her heart beat faster. But now she must do the shopping for her aunt.

"I'll be back soon," she said, then placed the list in her purse, checking first to make sure she had her car keys before leaving the kitchen and hurrying down the hall to open the front door. She stepped out into the slanting rays of late afternoon sun and drew a deep breath of the pungent sweetness wafting from the wisteria blossoms, hanging like purple grapes on the trellis beside the porch . . .

She stopped, expelling her breath in an explosive gasp when she saw Shaun leaning casually against the fender of his car out by the curb. For a moment she thought her mind was playing a trick on her—he couldn't be here, he had to be the product of her wishful thinking.

Then he lifted one hand and ran it through his hair until the curls stood out like electrified coils, and she knew she wasn't imagining it. Love for him surged through her in a rolling wave, almost sweeping her away. She ran down the steps and across the yard, wanting to fling herself into his arms; but just before she reached him, she slowed. His eyes, as blue as the Sweet William blooming brightly in one corner of the yard, held her with a look so concerned, so tender, that once again she felt her strength give way.

"I couldn't stand it any longer," he said softly. "If you're okay—well, I'll drive right back and not get in your way. But that's what I have to know . . . *are* you all right?"

She felt the dawning of a warm light in the very center of her being, a light that rose rapidly to permeate every fiber of her body and finally to push up the corners of her mouth in a wide smile, a sunrise of joy.

"Yes, more all right than I've ever been! My mother—well, we've worked it out, we're friends now. Oh, Shaun, you were right, I had to forgive her, not just for her sake, but for my sake, too! All that anger that was inside me . . . I never believed anyone could ever really love me." She paused, feeling the joy sweep through her once more. "When I forgave my mother, and asked her forgiveness . . . "

"*Her* forgiveness?" Shaun exclaimed.

Bethany nodded. "Shaun, there was a side to her story I never knew—because I never bothered to find out. I just considered everything from my own viewpoint. But when we forgave each other—it was as though I had broken free from invisible bonds, as though I could breathe and feel again. In learning to forgive—well, in learning that, I think, at last, I've also learned how to give love and . . . and how to accept love, from others, from . . . "

She had started to say, " . . . from you," but she paused, suddenly shy. All the things she wanted to tell him danced eagerly in her mind—that she loved him more than life itself, that he was the finest, the noblest, the handsomest, the most wonderful man she'd ever met. The words churned about inside her bubbling to get out, and yet they seemed to catch in her throat, piling up behind one last barrier of doubt— what if he didn't want her any longer, what if she'd come into this awareness of love's meaning too late?

But the look in his eyes, the dawning of hope as he seemed to read in her own face the words she couldn't speak, removed that final doubt. She plunged down, down, through the endless depths of those two blue pools, sensing at last the full range of his emotions, all the way from tenderness to volcanic desire.

The need to touch him, to hold him, to bridge that last remaining distance between them became more than she could bear. With two quick strides, she reached his side. He opened his arms to receive her and she entered that embrace with the rejoicing of a lost traveler who has found the way home. A warm glow suffused her body when he lowered his lips to hers, melting away the lead of old pain and transforming it into golden happiness.

At last, pausing to breathe, he pulled back from the kiss and pressed his cheek against hers. His words, a whisper of warm air caressing her ear, seemed to rise from the very depths of his soul: "I've loved you for so long!"

"I know." And she did know, with a certainty that warmed her like a fire. "I love you, too."

They stood for a long time, just holding each other. Finally he pushed her away at arm's length to remark with a wry grin, "I forgot this is a small town. What will your neighbors think, seeing you carry on like this in broad daylight?"

She grinned back, so buoyant with happiness that she seemed to float two feet above the sidewalk. "It will give them something to talk about for days."

"Well, I won't risk damaging my future wife's reputation any further." He released her but continued to hold her with his eyes, a visual embrace so strong she could almost feel it wrapping her about in loving warmth.

His future wife!

Her spirit soared at the thought, like a bird in flight, and she had a flashing vision of a white dove released from the fragile temple of a sand dollar to carry to the world the message of God's healing love. For it was indeed God's love that had brought her to this moment. She knew without a doubt, God worked through Shaun to teach her forgiveness and to lead her—not always gently, but always with love—to this moment of glorious joy.

Thank You, Lord, she called in silence, sure that He must be listening and rejoicing, too.

For one brief instant she seemed to feel the brush of wings against her cheek and to hear the call of a dove.

ABOUT THE AUTHOR

MADGE HARRAH is the prolific author of hundreds of articles, radio dramas, and novels. In addition, a student of the late Rod Serling, she is a prize-winning playwright. Not only is she proficient in prose writing—she is also a composer, song lyricist, and illustrator of children's books. It should come as no surprise, therefore, that in 1981 Madge Harrah was named one of only four women from a roster of 6000 members of the National League of American Penwomen to qualify for membership in three categories—writing, composing, and illustrating.

Of particular interest to our readers is Mrs. Harrah's contributions to *Guideposts* daily devotional guides for the years 1983, 1984, and 1985.

Despite all her credits, Madge maintains an exemplary humility. "I have eleven drawers of rejected manuscripts," she admits candidly. "I have aimed far higher than I have achieved. But you have to learn how to shift gears, to keep going, no matter what."

Madge Harrah is proof positive that such prayerful persistence is rewarded.

A Letter To Our Readers

Dear Reader:

Pioneering is an exhilarating experience, filled with opportunities for exploring new frontiers. The Zondervan Corporation is proud to be the first major publisher to launch a series of inspirational romances designed to inspire and uplift as well as to provide wholesome entertainment. In order that we might better contribute to your reading enjoyment, we would appreciate your taking a few minutes to respond to the following questions and return to:

> Anne Severance, Editor
> The Zondervan Publishing House
> 1415 Lake Drive, S.E.
> Grand Rapids, Michigan   49506

1. Did you enjoy reading CALL OF THE DOVE?
   - ☐ Very much. I would like to see more books by this author!
   - ☐ Moderately
   - ☐ I would have enjoyed it more if _____

2. Where did you purchase this book? _____

3. What influenced your decision to purchase this book?
   - ☐ Cover
   - ☐ Title
   - ☐ Publicity
   - ☐ Back cover copy
   - ☐ Friends
   - ☐ Other _____

4. Please rate the following elements from 1 (poor) to 10 (superior).

☐ Heroine   ☐ Plot
☐ Hero   ☐ Inspirational theme
☐ Setting   ☐ Secondary characters

5. Which settings would you like to see in future Serenade Serenata Books?

_____   _____

_____   _____

6. What are some inspirational themes you would like to see treated in future books?

_____   _____

_____   _____

7. Would you be interested in reading other Serenade Serenata or Serenade Saga Books?

☐ Very interested
☐ Moderately interested
☐ Not interested

8. Please indicate your age range:

☐ Under 18   ☐ 25–34   ☐ 46–55
☐ 18–24   ☐ 35–45   ☐ Over 55

9. Would you be interested in a Serenade book club? If so, please give us your name and address:

Name _____

Occupation _____

Address _____

City _____ State _____ Zip _____

Serenade Serenata Books are inspirational romances in contemporary settings, designed to bring you a joyful, heart-lifting reading experience.

Serenade Serenata books available in your local bookstore:

#1   ON WINGS OF LOVE, Elaine L. Schulte
#2   LOVE'S SWEET PROMISE,
      Susan C. Feldhake
#3   FOR LOVE ALONE, Susan C. Feldhake
#4   LOVE'S LATE SPRING, Lydia Heermann
#5   IN COMES LOVE, Mab Graff Hoover
#6   FOUNTAIN OF LOVE, Velma S. Daniels and
      Peggy E. King.
#7   MORNING SONG, Linda Herring
#8   A MOUNTAIN TO STAND STRONG,
      Peggy Darty
#9   LOVE'S PERFECT IMAGE, Judy Baer
#10 SMOKY MOUNTAIN SUNRISE,
      Yvonne Lehman
#11 GREENGOLD AUTUMN,
      Donna Fletcher Crow
#12 IRRESISTIBLE LOVE, Elaine Anne McAvoy
#13 ETERNAL FLAME, Lurlene McDaniel
#14 WINDSONG, Linda Herring
#15 FOREVER EDEN, Barbara Bennett

Serenade Saga Books are inspirational romances in historical settings, designed to bring you a joyful, heart-lifting reading experience.

Serenade Saga books available in your local bookstore:

#1 SUMMER SNOW, Sandy Dengler
#2 CALL HER BLESSED, Jeanette Gilge
#3 INA, Karen Baker Kletzing
#4 JULIANA OF CLOVER HILL,
   Brenda Knight Graham
#5 SONG OF THE NEREIDS, Sandy Dengler
#6 ANNA'S ROCKING CHAIR,
   Elaine Watson
#7 IN LOVE'S OWN TIME,
   Susan C. Feldhake
#8 YANKEE BRIDE, Jane Peart
#9 LIGHT OF MY HEART, Kathleen Karr
#10 LOVE BEYOND SURRENDER,
   Susan C. Feldhake
#11 ALL THE DAYS AFTER SUNDAY,
   Jeanette Gilge
#12 WINTERSPRING, Sandy Dengler
#13 HAND ME DOWN THE DAWN,
   Mary Harwell Sayler
#14 REBEL BRIDE, Jane Peart
#15 SPEAK SOFTLY, LOVE, Kathleen Yapp

Watch for other books in both the *Serenade Saga* and *Serenade Serenata* (contemporary) series coming soon:

#17   THE DESIRES OF YOUR HEART, Donna F. Crow (Serenata)

#17   THE RIVER BETWEEN, Jacquelyn Cook (Saga)

#18   TENDER ADVERSARY, Judy Baer (Serenata)

#18   VALIANT BRIDE, Jane Peart (Saga)